I0571811

1

All characters in this book are fictional. Any resemblance to actual persons, living or dead, is coincidental.

All rights reserved. This is protected under the copyright laws of the United Kingdom. Any reproduction or unauthorised use of the material or art work contained herein is prohibited.

Distributed worldwide by Writer's Sanctum Publishing LTD

Cover art by: Writer's Sanctum Publishing

ISBN: 978-1-9998786-5-8

First Print: 23/07/2018

Visit our Website: www.writerssanctumpublishing.co.uk

To Lesley, as always,

and to Phil, the voyager

The Intersection
by
Edmund Lester

Sunday September 3rd 2017, Alghero, Sardinia

Ben Williamson ducked into the small antique shop to escape the rain. It was just his luck for the heavens to open on the one day he'd left his raincoat back in the hotel room. Gilly had called back for him as he went to leave, suggesting he take it on his walk just in case. He'd just laughed and told her they weren't in England anymore. You didn't have to worry about the weather here the way you did at home. He was wrong.

He stood half in and half out of the shop, beneath the little awning over the entrance. The sky, bright and blue when he began this walk was now covered over in the darkest clouds. The rains looked to have settled in. Going back out there now would see him getting soaked to the skin. He would give it some time and hope it was just a shower. He knew it would not be though.

He turned away from the exit and peered into the shop. It was gloomy. There were not many lights and the window was mostly obscured by the piles of old suitcases the shopkeeper had erected. If it wasn't for the lack of anywhere else to put them Ben might almost have thought it a deliberate act to prevent light reaching the interior. Could the owner of the shop be a vampire? Ooh, scary.

Ben's eyes slowly became accustomed to the low level of light. Once he could see detail he was amazed. The shop was crammed. There was so much stuff in such a small space. The space where he was standing, on the doormat just inside the entrance might just be the only place where something hadn't been placed. The narrow alleyways between the wardrobes, cabinets and other dark wooden furniture were cluttered with an amazing array of knick-knacks; most of which Ben had no clue as to their original function.

To get through to the back of the store he would need to step over any number of small, old and probably very fragile items; all, no doubt, on a 'you break it, you buy it' basis. And that was before you counted the number of things suspended from the ceiling. The owner certainly hadn't made this an inviting place. Nevertheless with the rain seeming to get even more intense outside he needed to find something to occupy his time; and prevent the shopkeeper from throwing him out.

It would be no revelation to the man if he found out Ben was only here to escape the weather but he should at least pretend he might buy something. And he guessed there was always the chance he might find something for a few Euros that could fit inside his suitcase. Despite not being much of a collector, he did have one cabinet in his office back at home that he would put those little items he'd found irresistible over the years. Mostly they were junk, and Gilly had tried to get him to throw them away many times over, but whenever he picked one of them up the memory of where he'd bought it would return to him and he would be happy. He could never part with a single one and, in truth, Gilly knew that.

~*~

Ben looked out of the window again. It seemed to have stopped raining. That was good. He'd just about scoured every corner of the antique shop. Loitering much longer and he would have to start paying the shopkeeper rent. He nodded his thanks to the man behind the counter and headed for the door. That's when he saw it.

He had no idea why it had caught his eye. It certainly wasn't shiny. Quite the opposite, it was flat, round and made of dull metal. He had no idea why he'd even seen it. He thought about reaching for it; even moved his hand slightly in its general direction. But then he hesitated. His brain tried to fight off his need for trinkets. He didn't need it, and he certainly didn't need the 'Oh God, not another one' from Gilly.

His logical side told him to leave it. He dismissed the box and reached the handle. As he pulled the door open though something stopped him stepping through it. He needed to know if it was what he thought; if only to assuage his curiosity. After all just confirming it was what he thought it was – an old film canister – didn't mean he had to buy it.

He picked the item up.He was right in his guess. This was definitely an old film canister. He should then have put it straight back where he found it. But he didn't. He turned it over in his hands.There was a label on the underside with three words scrawled on it. Through the dust and the fading of years he struggled to read them. He held it up above head height to catch the little light that made its way passed the shop contents.

'L'Intersezione, New York' – *The Intersection*, New York. That was intriguing. Beneath it was a date – 1909.

'Attualità,' came a voice from the back of the shop. Ben was startled to hear him speak. He'd pretty much forgotten he was even there. He stared towards the man. 'Attualità,' he said again.'Il film.'

Ben puzzled the Italian in his head. He assumed it translated as 'Actuality'. He said the word aloud, 'Actuality?'

The shopkeeper must have taken this as a question. 'Si, si, Signore.Attualità,' he replied before adding,'E non e caro.' – *And it's not expensive.*

Ben had heard that line many times before. He thought it a shame for the man that he was firm on the amount he would spend on his trinkets and he could see no way this would be less than his maximum. 'Quanto?' he asked. – *How much?*

'Trenta euri,' came the reply. – *Thirty euros.*

Not a lot of money, just a little more than he'd want to have paid for an empty film canister he still wasn't totally sure he wanted. 'Venticinque?' he asked. – Twenty five.

'Si, si,' the shopkeeper replied. Before Ben could even think twice the man was wrapping the canister in newspaper and putting into a carrier bag. What had he done? Too late to worry now, he guessed. He handed the money over and headed back into the light beyond the door. What would Gilly think? Another one of his useless trinkets, no doubt. At least she wouldn't go on about it too long. She accepted his weird magpie tendencies; tolerating them as long as they stayed within his office or the basement. The rest of the house had to stay with her minimal preferences.

Ben fished his sunglasses from his pocket. The clouds had departed the sky leaving this corner of Sardinia bathed once more in warm sunshine. The pavements sparkled with the reflection of the sunlight on the small puddles of rainwater. This was an idyllic place. He headed back along Lungomare Dante towards the old city and their hotel, choosing the long route along the sea wall on Bastioni Colombo.

Gilly wouldn't mind the extra few minutes this would add to his walk. He knew exactly where she would be – sitting in the old cloisters that formed part of the hotel, reading her latest book. He laughed to himself at the put on disapproving look the carrier bag would receive.

Having bought it he actually felt more comfortable within himself. It would give him a new hobby for a few weeks upon his return to Solihull. He felt like researching 'L'Intersezione, New York'. What kind of film was it? And what exactly was Attualità?

Sunday September 10th 2017, Hockley Heath, Solihull

Ben Williamson had all but forgotten about the old canister. He'd put it in his suitcase when he got back to the hotel, having run the gauntlet of his wife's jokey nagging. And there it had stayed with not a single thought cast its way until he unpacked his case on Saturday evening. As expected, Gilly had ordered it into his office, standing and holding out her hand; indicating its banishment. He'd carried it mock shamefully into his office, placed it on the settee at the back of the room in front of the bookcase and once more it would lie forgotten.

His eyes had caught sight of it this as he entered his office to catch up on his emails and work a little on some of his private clients. It had brought a smile to his face, reminding him of his escape from a Mediterranean thunder storm and the beauty of Alghero in general. And a second later his mind was on work. That impulse holiday for the two of them, after dropping Naomi back at boarding school, may have been wonderful but now he would need to earn the money to pay for it.

Fortunately he had enough private work coming in to keep him busy until New Year. And from the number of emails he saw filling up his inbox that may well be extended until Easter. That would put Gilly's mind at rest; she had been a little concerned about the cost when he'd suggested the holiday.

Ben let the machine continue downloading and headed to the shelves of CDs. He needed some music to work to. What would today's choice be? He needed something rocky this morning; but not too much. He settled on the Rolling Stones' Exile on Main Street, hit the play button and started deleting the spam emails that had made their way through his filter.

His feet were tapping along with Charlie Watts' simple but effective drumming as he began to flick through the various client folders. He needed an easy one to get him back into the swing of things and there it was; annual returns for Smith Brothers. He grabbed his pen and notebook and started work. Through the speakers Mick Jagger was singing about Tumbling Dice over Keith Richards' wonderful guitar. He'd made the right choice with the music for today.

Four hours later and he felt he deserved a break. He stretched his arms backwards over his head, feeling the cracking of his joints; the perils of getting old. He grabbed his mug of tea, still barely warm enough to be drinkable, and headed for the sofa at the back of the room. He needed some down time before starting on the next set of accounts.

He moved the canister along on the sofa, thought for a second about picking it up and examining it further but quickly dismissed the idea. He knew what he needed at this moment. He reached for the acoustic guitar he kept there for just such emergencies. Resting it on his knee he flexed his fingers once or twice and then started picking out some tunes on the guitar.

He was happy. He felt relaxed. He enjoyed his life; even if he had to work most Sundays to keep up the payments on their daughter's schooling. It wasn't as though his job was arduous; you don't get bravery awards or danger money to be an accountant. The severest danger he was probably in was the risk of a paper cut.

He finished his tea, wincing slightly. It had gotten too cold but he felt bad about wasting it. He glanced at his watch; one pm. Gilly would be calling him in for lunch soon. Would he have time enough to do anything productive back at the computer? Probably.

He replaced the guitar on its stand and went to stand. As he did so, his hand brushed the dull metal canister. The coldness surprised him. He halted his rising and lifted it from the seat cushion once more. It was an odd thing. And it was heavy; heavier than he expected. He was surprised he hadn't noticed the weight of it when he bought it.

Ben remembered the label underneath and flipped it over again. Something inside the canister moved. That surprised him. He hadn't thought anything was inside it when he'd bought it. He certainly hadn't factored contents into the decision on the price. He'd paid twenty five Euros, under twenty pounds, for the canister and had considered it a fair price. If it contained anything it was a bonus.

He turned the canister on its side and searched for a release mechanism. His fingers were just settling on the clip when Gilly opened the door. 'Dinner will be ready just after two,' she said.

He glanced at his watch again. That gave him an hour. That was enough to get back to work.The canister went back onto the seat cushion forgotten yet again and he was on his feet heaving back to the computer, via the short delay to select the next CD – Queen's Innuendo, a much underrated album in his opinion.

He'd completed all the easy jobs already. He cursed himself for not being brave enough to tackle something earlier. He would have to do it now – tax accounts, nobody's favourite. He wouldn't be able to finish this before Gilly announced food was ready; in fact he was not going to get this done today at all. He would have to work an evening or two on this. At least it would bring in a decent fee. And Gilly would be out at art class on Tuesday so he wouldn't feel too guilty about it seeping into the week.

Sunday 17th September 2017, Hockley Heath, Solihull

The canister had lain forgotten again for another week. And to add insult to injury this morning when he walked in after breakfast he'd not even noticed it.Not entirely surprising really;it didn't exactly make an effort to draw attention to itself. Not like the four Scandinavian coloured glass vases he kept on the window sill. They sparkled as the light shone through them. They'd been his highest ever costing impulse purchases on holiday. He wandered over and picked up the largest piece; a bamboo vase by Finnish glass maker Riihimaki. It was a wonderfully wacky piece and he loved it. It made him smile every time he entered the room.

He remembered the day when he'd bought them. On the advice of a Dutch former colleague he'd headed over to Holland for Koninginnedag, *Queen's Day*, some years back. He'd chosen Nijmegen as it seemed close enough for them to head into Germany a little on the same trip.

Holland had been so much fun they'd never made it to Germany. The Dutch threw a great party for their national day. It had actually made him ashamed to be British. St. George's Day had gone mostly unnoticed back at home just a week before. It had only been the evening when he saw a report on the local news that he'd even realised the significance of the date.

The Dutch though, were never going to miss theirs. They had multiple stages erected around the city centre with rock bands and DJs leading the partying – which had of course started the day before. It had been a revelation.

But it was the morning that had seen the four vases enter his collection. They'd been told what to expect on the morning of Queen's Day; a car boot the like of which you would not believe if you hadn't seen it. Well even after having seen it he still hadn't believed it. It stretched all across the park by the sport's arena and further; snaking through several of the adjoining roads. It was astounding. And it had been where he'd seen the glass vases.

He'd been instantly besotted with them and barely bartered the seller down from the two hundred and eighty Euros he'd asked. Ben had only managed a twenty Euro discount before desperately handing over his money; so keen was he on not missing out on owning them.

That was the one time Gilly's disapproving look at his crazy purchases had been serious. It had taken a fair while to mollify her. But they were worth it. And from the fact Gilly had even allowed two of them in lounge for a while told him she liked them too.

As he replaced the vase carefully on the window sill his thoughts returned to the canister he'd bought in Alghero. He switched on the computer, set his email downloading and headed straight for the sofa.

~*~

Ben flicked the catch to release the lid of the canister and opened it. What was inside surprised him greatly; even though on reflection it was the most obvious of contents for a film canister. Inside there was a reel of film. What else would there have been?Ben felt a little foolish at being surprised.

He lifted it out of the canister carefully; not carefully enough though. The end of the film fell out of the reel and hung down. He quickly stopped it all unspooling. He wound it back onto the reel. As he did so the light from the window caught it.

The film had a definite brown tinge but was intact. Ben had almost expected it to be dust after a century and more. He held the frames up to the light to see the images. What he saw was fascinating and very much in keeping with the Italian word written on the label - L'Intersezione, *The Intersection*. The image was precisely that, a road junction. He presumed it was New York; he had no reason to doubt the rest of the label. But it wasn't a scene he recognised.

He carefully unrolled more of the film looking at the scene as he did. The camera didn't seem to have moved at all. It was just capturing life in front of where the cameraman had placed it. Maybe that's what the shopkeeper back in Alghero had meant by 'Attualità'. Was this real life? It seemed odd to Ben. But he was from a different time. He'd grown up with movies and television being ubiquitous; and getting more so by the day.

But a century ago it would not have been the case. Ben couldn't even be sure radio had been around when this film was shot. He had a feeling it was a Victorian invention. Victorians seemed to have invented or discovered everything about modern life; even computers saw their origins in that era with Charles Babbage. So would the early twentieth century have been enough time to set up radio broadcasting? Possibly; possibly not. He'd need to head over to Wikipedia for the answer.

He soon stopped unrolling the film, worried about damaging it. He wouldn't mind seeing the film contained on the reel but without a projector he knew it was unlikely. And in any case, he had work to do. He rewound the film onto the reel, stowed it back in its canister and headed to his computer. He had had distraction enough today; he needed to get on.

On a whim Ben loaded up ebay during his break from working. He'd gotten ahead over the past couple of weeks with his private clients and had more than enough to pay for the next two payments on Naomi's education. So he'd decided to maybe have a hunt online for some Christmas presents; get them done and dusted quickly.

He thought of his brother, Tom. Tom was a mad David Bowie fan and luckily for Ben had loaded the list of his entire collection onto the cloud. Ben had requested the password for their account with the excuse of being able to download the videos of his nephews that occupied the family part of his uploading. The truth was though he wanted to get him something truly special this year.

It would be Tom's fortieth birthday on Boxing Day and he'd always felt Tom missed out; too many relatives had handed over presents when they were kids with the tagline 'It's for your birthday as well'.Ben had always found it a cheapskate thing to do. It wasn't as though they spent any more than they would have on just a Christmas present. Ben had vowed he would never do that to his kid brother.

He typed in Bowie Starman to the search and hit search. Maybe he would find a variant of the single, his brother's favourite, that he didn't already own. The first few were all standard, nothing unusual. The only surprise of the first page was a listing for an old science fiction with the lead story 'Starman Come Home'. Not what he was looking for.

He continued through a few more pages before giving it up as a bad idea. He changed his tack and found a listing for a still open record store in Southampton. He fired off an email requesting details of any unusual Bowie items and decided to wait on its response. He had time. There were still two and a half months until Christmas and Tom's birthday after all.

He was just about to close down eBay and get to work when he noticed an image of a digital camera on eBay's home page – one of the items it was recommending to him, probably based on some of the weird items he'd browsed or bought over the years. It wasn't something he wanted. These days he had camera enough for him in his smart phone. But it reminded him of the canister still lying on the seat cushion behind him; he'd never got around to putting in the cabinet with his other impulse buy trinkets and oddities.

He still had the desire to watch the film it contained. He wanted to find out what happened in L'Intersezione. Was it a film as he knew it, with actors, plots and many different scenes? Or was this literally a recording of a street junction in New York City? Without a projector he would never know.

But how do you search for that? Was there just one format? Would any projector of the period do the job, or did he need to find the precise one for his film? He typed 'Antique Film Projector' in eBay and hit search again. What was returned confirmed his fear.

There were a number of old projectors on the list; although many were obviously nowhere near the age of his film. Mid-Century seemed to qualify as antique; odd. And there seemed to be a number of different formats mentioned –9.5mm; 16mm; 35mm; Super 8 all featured multiple times – as well as a number of listings that made no mention whatsoever of a format. They were obviously being sold as decorative pieces only. He wasn't sure he would find out anything more. He needed to get advice on it. And he knew just where to start – after all what isn't on Google?

A trawl of local antiques dealers had occupied the remainder of his morning; work had not even been a consideration. He'd called up several of the phone numbers trying to see if any were open on a Sunday. Many were; a popular day for the trade he guessed with people not at work. But they mostly knew little about the operation of the kind of projector he needed. They were selling them as objects only.He was just about to give up, but decided to try one more number.

'John Dean Antiques, how can I help you?' the voice asked.

'Hello, I'm hoping you can help me. I'm looking for an antique film projector. I bought an old film reel and I would love to watch the film it contains.'

'I'll do my best. Can you tell me what format it is?'

'I'm sorry,' Ben replied, 'but I have no idea of how to ascertain that.'

'Have you measured it?'

'Measured what?'

'Okay, I see.' Ben could tell the man must think him dumb.

'I'm sorry. I really don't know what I am looking for. Can I ask whether you are open today? I could bring my film along and let you see it and then give me some advice.'

The dealer readily agreed; maybe just to get the idiot of the other end of the phone line quickly. Ben asked him for directions to his shop, in a village just south of

Stratford. He was open until four pm. Ben looked at his watch. He had three and a half hours. That should give him far more than enough time; it was only a thirty minute drive after all.

Unfortunately for Ben, the moment he put the phone down Gilly opened the door. She was about to serve dinner. He wouldn't be able to leave for at least an hour; maybe more if his wife had cooked a desert. He smiled despite his disappointment and told her he would be straight out.If he had given any sign of his annoyance at her timing, she had not seemed to notice. That was good. He didn't want to cause an argument.

He turned his attention to his emails – not even looked at so far. Most were the usual variety of rubbish – circulars from various accountancy groups he'd stupidly given his email address to; money off vouchers from a pub whose food he found disgusting; discount offers on stationery and updates on postings on Facebook or Twitter. How much worse would that have been had his spam filter not filtered out most of the phishing emails; PPI claims advice and various pharmaceutical offers?

At the end he was left with just six emails he actually wanted; three of which looked likely to lead to more private clients. He responded to each of them and added three new folders to his filing system before heading for the dining room and lunch with Gilly. He prayed it would be short enough to let him head out to John

Dean's. He'd use the excuse of needing to visit a client to collect some paperwork. She wouldn't question it.

Sunday October 1st 2017, Newbold on Stour, Warwickshire

The visit to John Dean antiques had gone as well as Ben could have expected. John had turned out to be a specialist in early film and radio as well as other early technologies. His shop, only open for a few weeks, was crammed to the rafters with all manner of early cameras with expanding bellows, Bakelite radio sets and various items of engineering equipment.

John too had proven a very pleasant and chatty man. He got Ben's interest wholeheartedly and, like Ben, was also married to a woman who did not. The two of them hit it off immediately.Ben felt like he'd known him for years. He even asked if they'd met before. John just put it down to his having one of those faces.

Whatever the reason though, Ben felt instantly at home with the guy. He trusted him from the off. So much so he handed over his prized possession without a worry in his head. He watched as John extracted the reel from the canister.

'Ah, you've got an old Actuality Film,' he said.

'That's what the guy in Sardinia said when I bought it,' Ben confirmed. 'But I had no idea what it meant.'

'Sardinia, eh?' John mused. 'That explains the Italian. I take it the word means Intersection.' He looked to Ben for confirmation. Ben nodded. 'Well, an Actuality film is pretty much what it says on the tin. Early film makers used to just set up their cameras anywhere they felt like and let them run.'

'So there was no plot or acting?' Ben asked.

'No, none whatsoever. There was no need for it. The film makers would roll into town, find what looked like popular location and shoot maybe ten minutes of footage. They would just capture scenes of everyday life then set up showings to a paying audience, usually made up of the people they'd just filmed wanting to see themselves in the film.'

'Plots or structure of any kind were unnecessary. The novelty of a moving image was enough to capture people's imagination, and of course cash, in those days. You need to consider that this is not much more than ten years after the first moving picture camera was even invented. These things were incredibly rare back then.'

'So does that mean I'm not going to be able to find a projector?' Ben asked despondently.

'Oh no, far from it. The format you have is pretty normal. It's an early 35mm; that format was the dominant one for decades. You shouldn't have a problem getting something to play your film on.'

'Do you have any?' Ben asked.

'Of course I do. I wouldn't be much of a specialist if I didn't. Although most of these in here are for talkies. Your film is twenty years before that. I do have one that will probably be suitable – it'll look the part too. It's an old Keystone Moviegraph from the twenties; a little after the film but not far out. It's a lot cheaper than trying to get one from the Edwardian period. Mind you it will only do if you don't mind hand cranking the film. This thing isn't electric or anything fancy.'

'That doesn't worry me. Can you tell me which one it is?'

'It's not in the shop yet. I've only just got hold of it and it's in the back. I'll just go get it for you.' With that John headed through the curtain to the room beyond.

~*~

Ben couldn't contain his disappointment when John returned. He'd been expecting something looking like the iconic old movie projector – two reels feeding a film between them and a light shining from the front. This was a dull grey metal box, rectangular in shape sitting on its shorter side. The only clue he had to its purpose was the lens at the front.

'Hey, don't give up on this so quickly. It'll look a lot better when I get the arms to hold the film reattached and tidy it up generally. It's in farm fresh condition at the moment; I've not spent any time on it. I'll get the electrics sorted too.'

'That all sounds expensive,' Ben replied.

'Well it's not going to be a tenner, if that's what you mean. But this really is a great machine and when it's restored it will look a million dollars – although cost only a fraction of that.'

'How much?' Ben asked.

'Fully working, rewired and guaranteed – four hundred. And that comes with a few spare bulbs and a bunch of other early films. It's a bulk lot.'

'I'll take it,' Ben responded immediately, without thinking.

'That was an easy sell,' John replied. 'Well I'll reserve it for you with a small deposit. How does fifty pounds sound?'

'That's fine.' Ben fished five ten pound notes out of his pocket and watched as John hand wrote an invoice for the projector, noting his payment. A shake of the hands and it was all done.

Ben relaxed. He hadn't realised how tense he'd become. His neck muscles were aching. As John moved the projector back to his workshop behind the store he moved the conversation to general small talk. He asked Ben what he did for a living.

'I'm an accountant,' Ben replied. John laughed. 'What's so funny?' Ben asked.

'I've been meaning to look for one for months now. The guy I used to use retired in April and moved to Spain. This meeting looks as though it might be more mutually beneficial than either of us probably imagined.'

Ben slipped easily into work mode. He asked a few basic questions about how John ran his business, gave him some free advice and came away with another new client to add to the three his emails had contained. All this and he would soon be the owner of a vintage projector; not to mention a bunch of other old films. This was feeling like the beginning of another hobby; another one that would no doubt case Gilly to roll her eyes in mock despair.

He placed his briefcase containing the canister down on the passenger seat of his Audi. He was happy. He fished in his glove compartment for a CD to play on the return home. His hand came out with a CD-R another client had handed to him a week or more ago. Mr. Reuben was a talent agent and he was raving about this old band from the nineties called Domino Effect that had reformed and recorded a new album.

Reuben was convinced it was going to be massive. He'd thrust a CD-R into Ben's hand and told him to give it a listen, which Ben of course had completely failed to do. He hesitated, unsure of whether to give it a listen or not. Reuben's track record with this kind of thing had left a lot to be desired over the years he'd been Ben's client. But he guessed it wouldn't hurt to give it a try.

Ben slid the CD-R into the player and waited for it to start. Heavy keyboards, nice crunchy guitar chords; it sound a lot better than Ben had expected. Pleasantly surprised he closed up the glove box again and put his car into reverse. By the time he left Newbold and headed back towards Stratford the singer was already starting the second chorus and Ben was humming along; catchy song.

When Ben had received John's call about his projector he'd immediately booked the following day off work, inventing a family emergency. His colleagues at Diamond Associates were not the type to pry when no immediate detail was added to such a statement; even if Robyn on reception was desperate to know any piece of gossip she would never think of asking him to elaborate.

Old man Diamond had only asked how he was going on the Cookson account. When Ben had said everything was ahead of schedule and he was waiting for more information to arrive before he could continue there had been no hesitation in granting permission for his day off – even given the lack of notice. There was much to be said for working for a small company and putting in the work over many years.

Ben hadn't informed Gilly about his purchase or the day off he was taking to go collect it. It was her day to see her sister Ali so hopefully he would have the chance to get down to Newbold, pick up his projector, get home and have it set up in the basement before she got home. With the number of boxes down there he could just claim it was an old family heirloom or something like that, that he'd brought back when his mother had died.

Gilly had no idea what was in any of them so would be none the wiser.

Ben actually had butterflies in his stomach, so eager was he to get to see his newly restored purchase. For a whim purchase of a canister, not realising it had a reel inside, the thought of getting to see the film was almost intoxicating.

He decided against heading the one junction down the M42 to take the motorway to Stratford, deciding instead to take the more scenic route and savour the experience further. It was such a nice day, especially for October, that the thought of driving the old single carriageway road rather than the motorway was irresistible.

The decision though proved frustrating. There was an accident on the approach to Stratford; one he didn't spot until it was too late to find an alternate route. He was stuck. He switched off his engine as he watched the fire brigade and ambulance service work to free the young woman from the crumpled Ford Focus she'd been driving.

He was irritated by the delay.He tried to suppress the feeling and felt guilty for even having it. He wasn't usually so callous. On any normal day his first thoughts would have been with the poor unfortunate victim of the crash.Today though he was back to being like a kid in a sweet shop. The past ten days since he met John Dean and saw his projector, collecting it had never been far from the front of his mind.

Gilly had even commented on his being more distracted than normal; he would have to admit to having a tendency to wander off into his own thoughts. He'd made a quick excuse – mentioning the stress of the upcoming audit on the Cookson account and being tired. Gilly had looked him up and down trying to read his expression. After a few seconds, seemingly satisfied with it, she'd offered her sympathy, asked if there was anything she could do to help then changed the subject.

The truth was though that he wanted, no needed, to see the movie his Sardinian purchase contained so badly it was a constant distraction. It had been a real effort to push it from his thoughts.

Eventually there were signs of movement up ahead. A young policewoman began signalling some cars through. It would take a few minutes for it to clear enough for him to be passed the obstruction but at least he could see progress being made. He inched forward, car length by car length, towards the freedom of being passed the accident site. His mood was lifting. He started to hum along to the Domino Effect CD-R still in his CD player. It had really grown on him. Maybe Reuben's judgment for once had some basis in reality.

~*~

Ben almost cursed aloud when he reached John's store in Newbold. Here was a sign on the door 'Back in Fifteen Minutes.' it said. Damn, just his luck. He stared at his watch; ten twenty three. It was far too early for lunch; maybe the man had popped out to the post office or bank. He looked around the village. Did this village have either of those? A bank was unlikely in the extreme, but a post office? Well most villages had had them until a few years ago when the government had closed hundreds of them. He'd thought it a ridiculous decision then and hadn't changed his mind since; especially not as it might now be delaying him from his movie projector.

Ben looked up and down the street to see if he could see anywhere john might be. Apart from houses all he could see was a church, a pub he didn't know was still open and an interiors shop. The last one looked out of place.Had he seen a post office as he entered the village? He had a vague impression of there being a village shop towards the other end of the high street but whether it had a post office he had no clue.

His musings quickly became irrelevant. John opened the door from inside. 'Come on in,' he said.

It surprised Ben. 'I thought you were out,' he said pointing at the sign as he entered the shop.

'Oh, sorry,' John apologised. 'I must have left that there from yesterday lunchtime. Maybe that's why I had such a quiet afternoon.'

Ben saw what he was looking for immediately. John had placed the Moviegraph on the counter. Newly cleaned and polished and with the reels attached it looked so much better than the rusting box he'd seen ten days before. The grin that found its home on Ben's face grew wide.

John must have seen it. 'I take it you like it, then?' he asked.

'Oh God, yes,' Ben replied. 'It's beautiful.'

'I'm glad. I've loaded it up with one of the other old films I mentioned that come with it. Do you want to see it in action? I can show you how to operate it then.'

'Yes, please.'

Ben was back in kid in candy shop mode. Ben watched carefully as John fired the projector up. The light slowly came up to full brightness; in truth not all that great but in a darkened room it would suffice to let him watch L'Intersezione. The film John had selected for the demo showed an industrial scene. It looked like a factory gate with the workers walking out.

'It's probably best not to leave any one part of the film with the light on it for long,' John told him. 'The bulb this thing takes isn't the strongest or hottest in the world but with film this old you never know.' He began turning the handle and the film began to roll.

On the wall at the side of John's shop counter the image began to move. Ben moved closer to the image to see it more clearly. As the image moved, Ben saw hundreds of people, young boys of maybe twelve or thirteen years up to white haired, white bearded old men. They all looked tired. From what he remembered hearing of working conditions a hundred years ago, the people on the film had probably worked a ten or twelve hour shift – and in much harsher conditions that modern workers would.

But still you saw a sparkle in their faces when they saw the camera. There was an excitement about it. The boys would run up to the camera and wave enthusiastically. The older workers, while much more restrained still showed a fascination. Ben tried to imagine what seeing this image a few hours after it was shot would have been like for people who had grown up in a world without television or the internet.

The film ran for eight minutes and nothing changed of note. Okay the people passing by the view were different but they were all the same type. All wore suits despite the obvious arduous work shift they had just completed. Most had blackened faces and all wore hats; mostly flat caps. The hats were the most obvious difference over the hundred years that separated him from them. He would find it unusual to see someone now walking down a street with a proper hat on. These days it was all baseball caps and beanies.

As the last frames ran through the projector and the image turned white, Ben realised neither man had spoken a word since the film started. He stared at the shopkeeper, speechless. John laughed. 'I take it you like it,' he said. He turned the projector off and switched the shop lights back on.

'It's fantastic,' Ben replied. It was. There was no point claiming otherwise. And this was with one of the films John had. Ben desperately wanted to run his own film, L'Intersezione, through it. He almost asked John if he could fetch the film out of his car and run it through but something inside stopped him. That first viewing was going to be his and his alone. He didn't want to share it with anyone.

'Come over here and I'll show you how it works,'

Ben reached into his jacket pocket and fished out a notepad and pen. 'You came prepared,' John said.

Thursday October 12th 2017, Hockley Heath, Solihull

Ben slowly drove his car passed the entrance to his house. There was one point in the road where he would be able to see whether Gilly's car was there. He didn't want the excitement of his new purchase spoiled by more of her moaning.

He leaned across the passenger side of the car, trying to see the full way up the drive. It was…empty. Good, she must be out with Ali. He reversed his car up, and turned it into the drive. He glanced at his watch. It was two thirty. He had to be quick. Gilly could be home any second. He almost sprinted from the car to the front door, unlocked it and typed it the passcode for the alarm system before returning to the car.

He opened the boot and there it was; or rather there the box containing it was. John had done a thorough job packaging it to prevent damage in transit. It was another thing he liked about the man. Of course this bulky a box made carrying it into the house trickier but he'd rather have had that then risk breaking it before he could even use it.

He carried it down into the basement and put it on the work surface. He'd cleared the areaspecifically for this as well as ensuring it would have a clear path to the wall opposite where he intended to project the image.

Ben opened the box, removed the top layers of packaging. It was intact. It had survived the drive. He was tempted to set it up immediately. He was desperate to watch his film. But his excuse for Gilly would only work if he was in the office when she returned. When she asked why he was home, he was going to say he needed the peace and quiet away from the office to get some work done so would be working from home today. She wouldn't question it. It did however mean he would have to leave his treasured possession down her unused and still hidden in its box.Regretfully he climbed the stairs back into the main part of the house and turned out the light.

He was just in time. As he fired up his computer and Outlook began downloading his email, he heard Gilly's car crunching the gravel on the driveway. He quickly spread documents over the desk to back up his story and headed to the door to greet his wife.

The afternoon went better than Ben could have imagined. Despite his fears he found it relatively easy to get to work. The thought that what he would charge for the work he was putting in would cover the cost of the Moviegraph helped.

When Gilly called him in to eat, she looked sheepish. There was something she didn't want to say to him; it was obvious. He didn't pry. These things were better to leave with her. She would tell him when she was good and ready. He just hoped she would hurry up about it though. If she didn't just get on with it, it would make the meal rather tense. Fortunately she did.

Midway through serving the meal she told him she needed to go out that evening. She looked very sheepish about it. He art club had a special guest speaker coming and he couldn't make their normal Tuesday evening group so they had added an extra night.

Most of the time, Ben would have been annoyed with her for doing this. Not for her wanting to go out. He never liked stopping her pursuing her hobbies, but she had to have known about this for days, possibly weeks, and she'd not told him until the last minute. He could have had plans for them both tonight. This time it was a godsend. He couldn't wait for her to be gone so he could watch L'Intersezione.

He quickly reassured Gilly that it was okay; he didn't mind; she should go if she wanted to. He knew it would do little to correct her reticence to announce such things to him but that wasn't uppermost in his mind today. All he could think about was his film.

It brightened his mood dramatically. Gilly too seemed relaxed; once she got over the stress of breaking the news to him. The meal was one of the most enjoyable ones they'd shared in a long while. They laughed and joked as they hadn't in years. She was like the young girl he'd met in high school all those years ago; laughing and blushing in equal measure.

Despite it all though, Ben was only too happy to wave her goodbye as she headed for her art class. It was seven pm. He would have at least three hours until she returned home; more than enough time to set up his projector and watch his film.

He couldn't head straight for the basement though. First there was the annoying matter of the dishwasher; again their years old agreement. She cooked, he cleaned up. And if he left it for later he knew there was no chance he would remember before Gilly returned home. He raced through his chores as quickly as possible, not taking as much care as he might have done otherwise. And that was why the plate slipped from his hand, shattering across the kitchen floor.

He cursed aloud, something he would never have done if Gilly was still in the house. He should never have rushed; things like this always happened when he did. He opened the cupboard under the sink, fished out the dustpan and brush and began to clear up.

~*~

Ben was determined to have learned his lesson from his earlier lack of care when he reached the basement. An accident here would be so much worse than a simple broken plate; here it would be catastrophic.

He re-opened the box and carefully removed the packaging that had kept the projector safe. He went to reach in to lift the Moviegraph out but thought better of it. It was too awkward a height to guarantee its safety. He searched in his tool drawers instead for a Stanley Knife. The box would be sacrificed to protect the machine inside. That was its function after all.

He checked for the projector's wiring, ensured it was well away from the cardboard of the box and began sawing through the side. A minute or two of careful demolition and the projector was freed. Ben moved the last of the packaging material away and there it sat; in all its ninety year old, rusty glory.

Ben opened his notepad at the pages of notes he'd taken at John's shop earlier. He'd filled it with detailed instructions on assembly, disassembly and operation. He needed to. There was no user guide with this; that had no doubt been discarded decades before Ben's birth, and this was a device from way before the current age of intuitive design. Everything had to be done precisely correct or the whole would fail; or worse, break.

Half an hour after he entered the basement he was happy it was set up correctly. He stretched across and plugged his Keystone Moviegraph into the wall socket. John had done a fantastic job but somehow to Ben the shiny white plastic cable with its PAT Tested sticker looked very incongruous against the old metal casing. As long as it worked though, he thought.

He switched the lamp on, wanting to test it before loading a film. It slowly came up to full strength; still dim. He placed his hand where the film would pass. It was warm, but seemed cool enough. John had reassured him there should be a little heat here after all. Old style bulbs are not all that efficient.

He instinctively went to reach for L'Intersezione; but that seemed too big a risk. Okay, he'd seen John demonstrate using the machine earlier and all had seemed to be fine but to put his film in first of all was something he dared not do. There were just too many things that could go wrong. He might have lined up any of the cogs and gears just slightly off square and it could result in the film being shredded as it passed between the two reels. Far safer to use one of the extra reels John had thrown in as a bonus with the purchase of the projector for its maiden run.

Ben reached under the work surface to the box of reels he'd hidden down there earlier. He pulled out the first that came to hand. They didn't have labels like his Italian find, so he was taking pot luck as to contents. He loaded the film as John had shown him, switched on the lamp again and cranked it into position as the light brightened.

The scene that greeted him was as different to the early industrial slice of life as he could imagine. This time the filmmakers had set up their camera on a seafront and had captured the Edwardians at leisure. Everything looked so formal. The women all wore elaborate, floor length dresses and wore frilly, wide brimmed hats. Many carried parasols. The men mostly seemed to be wearing three piece suits and a variety of hates; bowlers, boaters and top hats among them.

The men and women, and equally well dressed children, paraded themselves in front of the lens in all their finery.Many tipped their hat as they passed, sending a greeting to him across the decades. It reminded Ben of the Passagiatta; that slow processing through the old towns and showing off the Italians do after work.

Ben marvelled at the difference you would see if you went to the same location and people watched in the twenty first century. There certainly wouldn't be a suit, never mind a three piece suit, anywhere in sight. Today it would be all shorts, tee shirts and beer guts; and it seemed all the poorer for it.

Ten minutes after he had started to crank the film the projected image turned white. Ben glanced at the machine. He'd been fearful the film had snapped; not worrying for the film itself but that the machine might somehow be responsible. Fortunately though, everything seemed fine. The film had just stopped abruptly, with no prior warning. Was this typical of these films? Did the makers just continue shoot until they had no tape left? John had warned him these Actuality films would seem very shoddy and amateurish in comparison to modern documentaries, but this was more (or rather less) than he'd expected. Never mind, the equipment does at least seem to be working, he thought.

Happy he was not about to destroy his Sardinian purchase he set about rewinding the film onto the original reel; another marked difference to modern tech. The closest Ben remembered using was the VHS player they used to own – and even that had the rewind automated, requiring only the click of a button. There was something oddly satisfying about doing the thing manually though. He felt more in touch with it.

Once completed, he knew it was time. He wasn't going to delay seeing L'Intersezione for another moment. He unclipped the canister lid and fetched the reel out. He felt edgy. This was the moment. He fastened the reel in place and pulled the end of the film out, attaching it to the second, and empty, reel. Once it was all in place he breathed out. He'd been holding his breath throughout the whole operation.

Everything was now ready. He switched off the main light again and spooled the film forward as the lamp warmed up. He was getting used to the operation already and managed to time reaching the first actual frame by the time the lamp was up to full brightness.

He watched attentively as the scene in front of him came into view. It confirmed both the title and the few clues he'd got looking directly at the film. This was a view of a crossroads, intersection in American speak. The film makers had obviously set up on one of the four corners, but back a little down one of the roads from the junction itself. Unfortunately in picking their location, they had obscured the view of the street signs. There were no clues on screen to the exact location they'd chosen – unless he could find something on the internet about the shops and other businesses in the frame. Maybe he could garner enough information to help him track down exactly where they were. But for now he would just watch it. He wanted to enjoy it this first time; he could do the work of analysing the scene during a later viewing.

There was much in the image that he recognised as typical New York. He'd seen so many movies and TV shows set in the city it was almost a second home even though he'd never been. There was something about the buildings that was just different to anywhere else. Even though there were none of the supertall buildings that would come later (construction of the Empire State Building wouldn't start for another twenty years after this film was shot) the city just seemed tall. No building in the shot had less than five storeys; one of them sported twelve and further in the background was what must have been one of the city's earliest skyscrapers. The base was out of sight but he guessed it was at least thirty storeys.

But it was the busy nature of the intersection that had fascinated Ben. It was obviously a commercial district. The ground floor of every building in view was occupied by stores of all varieties, all with shoppers continually going in and out.But it was the road itself that was the heart of the activity. It was packed with carts, both horse drawn and hand pulled; cable cars; early omnibuses and even a car or two.

The film had captured a real turning point in time; the old reliance on horses was in the process of being replaced with motorisation. His film makers could not have chosen a better time for him. Any earlier and everything would have been horse drawn, later and this street would have been awash with motorcars and trucks only. He wondered how short the crossover would have been.

It felt as though the film had barely started when the last frame passed through the projector and it was over. Ben was stunned. That had been incredible. He was absolutely hooked and felt privileged to have been given the chance to peer through a window into this forgotten world. He'd shared ten minutes of the lives of hundreds of people, most of whom would have been dead before Ben even took his first breath. It was a chilling thought.

He turned off the lamp to save the bulb. He only had a finite supply although John was looking out for more that would fit the projector. Even if that failed though he knew the projector could be adapted to use more modern bulbs. All would not be lost.

Ben carefully rewound the film onto its original reel and started watching it through a second time. There was just too much to take in in just a single viewing.

As if to confirm the thought, within thirty seconds of the image returning Ben noticed a theatre on the corner opposite to his vantage point. He didn't recall that being there the first time; odd. His attention must have been elsewhere. He scoured round the whole scene trying to see if anything else had been missed. Nothing else seemed so obvious so he started people watching.

The styles of dress were partway between the industrial and seafront scenes he'd watched earlier. The few women that passed by the camera all wore floor length dresses and bonnets and the men were mostly suited but there was none of the out and out finery of the holiday scene. These people were at work. When a jacket was absent from one of the men it was replaced with an apron.

On the far left side of the view was a newsstand, a small kiosk next to stairs, presumably leading down to a subway station. The number of magazines and newspapers adorning the front of it was incredible. Ben had thought that the proliferation of special interest titles that filled his local newsagent was a very recent phenomenon. He certainly couldn't remember the vast numbers being there when he was a kid. But here in front of him was an image of exactly the same from more than a century ago.He strained his eyes to see if he could make out anything of the titles on sale but there was just not the detail there to tell. It was disappointing. He wanted to know everything about this place.

Sunday October 15th 2017, Hockley Heath, Solihull

Ben's normal Sunday routine had been dropped totally today. He wasn't even making the pretence of doing any work. He was hitting the internet right from the get go. He'd watched his film a dozen times now. The last half dozen had seen him approaching his task of locating the scene geographically within New York in a highly methodical way; one anyone who knew him would not have been surprised at.

Each time he watched the film now he focussed all of attention on one small area. He's chosen the voice memos app on his phone to aid him as he didn't have both hands free to take notes in the old fashioned way. And in any case he liked the idea of using cutting edge tech to analyse one of the earliest films made.

He dictated everything he saw in each section of the images as it progressed; the shop and other business names; any advertising signs on the delivery wagons that passed by and the route header on the omnibus that passed through. Any of these could help him.

There was so much more to be seen in the film; he'd noticed but paid precious little attention to the various hawkers and tradesmen making their living on the pavement itself. For his initial purpose they would not help. Being itinerant they would likely have set up their stalls in many places across the city across the months and years.

It had been a frustratingly difficult task. For all the signs that decorated every part of the scene there were precious few naming the premises. They all advertised their wares first and foremost; hardware; malted milk, pipe tobacco; rooms for hire; typewriters; toasted sandwiches; bicycles; and almost a dozen varieties of beer, from names he recognised like Budweiser and Guinness to ones that were new to him like Rheingold and the wonderfully named Hell's Gate. He had no idea whether these companies were still going. He hoped so. He would like to try a glass of one in a bar somewhere near his Intersection at some point in the future.

But after numerous rewatchings – not a chore – Ben had a dozen store and business names to search for on Google. The first he typed in was Miss Weber's Millinery. He found pages of detail of this now defunct store. It had been located on West 22nd Street. He typed the location into Google maps. He was in the heart of Manhattan Island.

He typed in the second name – Hotel Marlborough. A new address came up in his search – it was on Broadway between 36th and 37th Street. He searched for this on a map. It was nowhere near Miss Weber's. It didn't make any sense at all. How could they be captured on the same film?

He tried the third name – P. Schiavone & Sons. No results this time that seemed to match what he was searching for but from the name and the other writing on the window reading Banca Italiana he guessed it would be in Little Italy. He even found an image of the shop front, looking very similar to the one on the film when he tried Googling Little Italy Stores 1910. A quick search showed that to be much further south than the others, several blocks below 1st street. He was confused; a confusion that only grew when the next two names returning results on West 66th Street and East 112th Street. They can't all be right.

Frustrated he closed Internet Explorer and leant back in his chair. Maybe he'd just misread what he saw. He resolved to watch the film again and make his notes again from scratch. It just wasn't going to be today unfortunately. After dinner he'd promised Gilly they could go round her sister and spend some time with her family. What he sacrificed for that woman. He hoped she appreciated it.

Sunday October 22nd 2017, Hockley Heath, Solihull

On both Tuesday and Thursday Gilly had been out pursuing her pointless hobbies; ten years attending art group and classes and she'd never sold a single painting in any of the group's shows - he'd have given it up long ago. Ben didn't complain. It gave him alone time; a chance to analyse his impossible film again.

He rewatched L'Intersezione more than twenty times, focussing, this time, far tighter than before. When he played back the recordings he was amazed to hear how similar to the previous set they were in every way but the one that mattered.

He described the same street merchants, often using the same phrasing. He was nearly word for word on the handcarts and delivery trucks that passed through the view during the ten minute length of the film. But when he came to detail the shop and business names not a single one matched his first set of viewings.

And it wasn't as though he was close. If he had said Adams the first time and Adamson the second, he would have understood his error; or Thomas for Thompson. These were the kind of thing that happened in translating from what he saw to what he might say. But these were Bartoli becoming Sieczewski, Matthews becoming Hildesheim. How could he have been so mistaken?

He replayed the recording from the first view to see where the errors might have been; he hoped he'd mislabelled each section. That would put his mind at rest. But he hadn't. The spreadsheet he had created transcribing the first set of voice memos matched his list precisely and correlated with the second run on exactly no occasions.

Ben Williamson was troubled. It was as though L'Intersezione wanted to keep its secrets from him. But that just didn't make sense.It wasn't possible. Old films just didn't change each time you viewed them. He had to have made a mistake. He brought up a new map of New York on his second monitor and began searching for the location of the intersection from the store names, just as he had a week before. And just as he expected the results he found didn't match.

In fact this time they made even less sense. At least the first time had seen all the results located on Manhattan Island. Today's grouping stretched further afield with two of the stores being located in the Bronx and one in Queens.

He needed to take a second look, which meant running the gauntlet that was Gilly. She always looked disapprovingly at him when he took any time off working on his private clients on Sundays. It was pissy of her to do so. It wasn't as though she worked any day of the week. She just sat on her arse most of the time and then got all judgmental when he needed down time.

There was nothing else for it though. He needed to watch it again and this time he would take his time, run the film slower and try to tick off the names on his list. He would see how many of them matched if he watched it today; from either list. It sounded insane but it was the only way he could think of sorting out the puzzle. One of them had to be right.

Impatiently he waited for the two sheets to run their way through his printer. As he did so the third possibility entered his mind. What if neither list contained a single business name that matched the film? He found the thought troubling.

~*~

Ben's fears were confirmed within thirty seconds of starting the film again. Where he had Bartoli or Sieczewski, he now saw Kelly Brothers; where he had hoped to find either Matthews or Hildesheim there was now Glovers' Butcher Shop.He considered watching it through again but feared the names would change yet again. He didn't think he could deal with that.

He switched off the lamp with the film only a third of the way through and dropped his hand from the handle. He was lost. This film had been his sole focus for the past few weeks but now the film was blocking him out. Had he upset it somehow? Had he done something wrong? He wished he knew, because then he would have a chance to put things right between them. He needed this film. He felt oddly lost without it.

He started to rewind the film and that's when it happened. He wasn't paying full attention to what he was doing; he was still working his way through his thoughts. He was about to start the third reverse rotation of the handle but hadn't noticed the reel had moved slightly off its spindle. The film jammed and then snapped.

His world froze. He just stared at the two jagged ends of film hanging down from each of the two reels. His brain tried to comprehend what it meant; what the swaying celluloid signified but he couldn't form a single coherent thought. It was as though someone had switched the major part of him off. When it all came back to him he wished they had. Numb was better.

Ben felt the desperation invade him. It was almost like a wave flowing into every part of his soul.He felt his temperature rise rapidly. His heart seemed to want to beat its way through his chest. It all sounded clichéd and the kind of thing he presumed you would read in second, no third rate, crime noir or romance novels. He dropped to his knees and began sobbing.

A few minutes later he heard the basement door open. 'Ben, are you okay down there?' He heard his wife's footsteps on the stairs leading down from the hallway above. Gilly was coming. He quickly rubbed at his eyes. She mustn't see him like this. He quickly reached across and pushed the nearby light switch to neither on nor off. It would prevent her switching the man light on and keep the room illuminated by the lamp on the work surface.

He heard the switch click into place. 'Oh, is the light out?' she asked.

'Yeah,' he replied. 'It blew when I came down here.'

'How did you find your way through all these boxes without breaking your neck?'

He pulled his smart phone from his top pocket. 'Torch app,' he replied.

Gilly nodded. She'd bought it. 'So what do you have down here?' she asked. 'What is that? Is it your latest hobby?'

'It's an old movie projector,' Ben replied. No point in denying what it was. It would only make her more curious.

'Was it amongst your mother's things?' she asked. Ben just shrugged. 'Does it work? Did she have any films?'

'A few; I just tried one but it snapped as I was rolling the film through.'

'What about the others? Would they be okay?'

'I guess they might be.'

'Could we watch one? I'm curious,' she asked.

It really was the last thing Ben wanted. There was only one film that Ben wanted to watch and that now lay ruined in pieces. And if he was to watch L'Intersezione or any of the other films he didn't want to watch them with her. This was his. 'I'm not sure it's working properly,' he said.

'Could we give it a try?' She gave him that mournful look; the one that had always seen him cave in to her wishes. It didn't have the same pull on his heart today. He didn't think it ever would again, but he couldn't let her know that.

'Okay,' he said. 'Just give me a few minutes to get the damaged film out of the reel.'

'Thanks. This'll be fun.' She looked at him carefully unspooling the damaged first section of L'Intersezione. 'I'll just go get the bin for you,' she said.

'No,' he said; rather too forcefully. The tone of his voice shocked her. 'Sorry,' he quickly added; his voice much softer this time. 'I want to see if it can be repaired.'

'Why would you repair it?' she asked. 'Isn't it just a dumb old tape?'

He blinked slowly and attempted to control his rage at her crass suggestion. 'This film is more than a hundred years old. It's an antique. I can't just throw away antiques.'

She gave him an odd look but didn't really say anything; just a huh. He ignored her and concentrated on removing his precious film without damaging it further. He glanced at his watch. It was two pm. If he could get Gilly out of here quickly enough, he would still have time to ring John. John might know someone who could fix his film.

~*~

Ben had the first dream that night. When he woke he wasn't sure where he was. The bedroom seemed superimposed with the Intersection. It took more than a minute for it to fade from his consciousness. He'd been there; in his dream. He'd walked those streets. He'd looked into the shop windows; watched the people moving about their everyday lives.

The dream didn't surprise him. He'd watched and rewatched the film more than thirty times since he bought it. If he was honest he was surprised he'd not dreamed about it before now. The undertone of the dream though, did. Something felt wrong. Everything was dirty. Windows were broken. Rubbish blew across the street. And more than one fight erupted on the street while he watched. None of that reflected the L'Intersezione.

He felt wrong.He pulled himself up to a sitting position, being careful to not rouse Gilly. He was wet and clammy; cold despite the relatively warm late October weather. He pulled the duvet up higher to try to get warm back into his bones. He thought about the dream. It seemed obvious what his subconscious was trying to tell him. He was guilty for breaking the film. He didn't really need his dreaming mind to make that clear. He felt guilty. His own brain showing him the intersection in a dishevelled, rundown condition, as though the damage he'd wrought on the old celluloid had transferred to the place itself.

He needed to get it fixed as soon as possible. Hopefully John today would have good news for him. He'd caught him yesterday in the process of shutting up his shop. John had listened to him for a few minutes then asked if he could call back in the morning. Regretfully Ben had agreed. He repeated his mobile number. He didn't want the call intercepted by Gilly. She would just question why he was *wasting* money on an old film no one cared about.

He felt like telling her exactly how much value he thought she'd gotten from years of art classes. He'd stopped himself just in time. Not out of compassion for her. He'd stopped caring about that. He just couldn't see it would do any good. She was trapped in her ways and he wasn't going to change her now.

He wasn't going to sleep again that night. There was no point trying. All he would do is toss and turn and wake Gilly. That was one conversation he could do without. He reached across for his smart phone and pulled up the BBC News app. He tried to distract himself with the headlines.

It didn't work. All he could think of was the film. He minimised the app and started at background screen. It was a picture of their daughter, maybe five years ago. She'd been a cute nine year old. He'd always found the image reassuring. Even in his darkest days, Naomi could make him smile. Not today.

He looked to the top of the screen. The time read four eighteen. It was two and a half hours before he could get up without raising suspicion. He searched desperately through the installed apps for some kind of distraction. Nothing worked.

'I don't normally come in on a Monday,' John said. 'But something in your voice told me you need me to.'

'Thank you for this,' Ben replied. 'I really do appreciate this.'

John looked him up and down. Maybe he'd let a little too much desperation to show through. He couldn't risk alienating this man. He was his only hope. 'Sorry, if I sound like a madman. Gilly wanted to watch it and I was careless. She threw a bit of a paddy and...you know.'

'Don't I?' John replied. That was too easy. He must have issues of his own at home. 'Now do you have that film?'

Ben reached into the plastic bag he carried and fished out the film. The jagged end fell down out of the reel. Ben winced as he saw it again. John took the reels from him and moved over to his shop counter. He studied both broken ends. 'You've been lucky,' he said. 'This could have been a lot worse.'

Ben didn't feel particularly lucky. 'How so?' he asked.

'Well, the film itself, barring the break obviously is undamaged. It must have sheared at a stress point. If it hadn't it could have twisted or stretched the rest of the film. This won't be too difficult to repair and you'll probably only lose six frames or so.'

'What effect will that have?' Ben asked.

'Huh?' John stopped inspecting the film ends. 'Oh, sorry. I was just working out how best to do this. The effect… It'll probably skip a little; you'll probably notice a split second jump but you won't lose much. Anyway I can have it fixed for you in a few hours.'

Ben felt immense relief it was saveable, but worried about the future. Both the film and the projector are a hundred years old. It was probably inevitable that this would happen again. He asked John for his advice going forward.

'Well, there is one way to prevent this kind of thing. I didn't mention it as it doesn't usual appeal to the kind of people who buy the old stuff. My customers tend to be purists.'

'I'm not,' Ben said, 'So you don't have to worry about upsetting me.'

'Good. Well you can have the film scanned. I know a place that will feed the film through their system and produce a DVD or Blu-Ray of the film for you; whichever you prefer. Then you can watch it on a modern player and not have to risk the film itself.'

That sounded perfect. 'Is the process dangerous? Could it damage the film further?'

'No, their equipment is a lot safer than the old projector. For one thing it uses a modern bulb; much less heat. It also has sensors that prevent the kind of force required that would break it again. And it would mean it only played once.'

'How long will that take?' Ben asked.

John hesitated a second. 'I can't say for sure. But it should only be a few days. They can usually find time to handle small jobs like this in between their other work. Do you want me to get you a quote?'

'No need,' Ben replied. 'I'll pay whatever they ask.'

'Don't let them hear that. The might just raise their rates,' John laughed. 'Don't worry though. I'll make sure they give you a good price. Leave the film with me and I'll get it over to them. It should be back with you by the weekend.'

Ben thanked him and left. He sat for a while in the car park before leaving Newbold. He was exhausted. The nervous energy that was keeping him going had disappeared. He leant back in the driver's seat of his car and fell asleep.

Sunday October 29th 2017, Newbold on Stour, Warwickshire

Ben had endured one of the worst weeks of his life. He felt as though he'd suffered one of the worst bouts of flu imaginable; just without the coldlike symptoms. The little sleep he had got over the past six days had done no good whatsoever.

His colleagues at work had all asked him if there was something wrong. Robyn on reception had been almost shaking when she'd asked. She'd thought he might have cancer or something like that. She always did go straight to the extremes. He had to admit he had looked a sight when she approached him. So bad even Gilly had asked if he was okay. That was something she rarely did.

It was all self-inflicted; just not through over indulgence. This was just his crazy brain making him suffer for what he'd done. He'd hoped that when his subconscious would have rewarded him with a peaceful night once he'd received word of the repair being complete, or the transfer to DVD was successful. It hadn't. He'd continued to lie for hours staring at his bedroom ceiling in the gloomy night light. He just hoped that today meant it was going to be all over.

He was going to be taking possession of the film back so he deserved a break. He'd feel better when he could watch it again. He'd tried to remember the faces of the inhabitants of the Intersection during his sleepless nights; but nothing came to him. He'd listened to many of the recordings he'd made during his watching; ignoring the commentary on the business and place names visible and concentrating on the people. But despite some occasionally very detailed descriptions, they trigger no visual recollection. He hoped it was just the tiredness he felt numbing his memory.

He needed to be let back into the world of his film. Last night his paranoia had run wild. He'd pictured the scene in John's shop – his current destination. He'd seen John take the newly written DVD, enter it into the drive on his PC, fire it up and kick the movie off. He could hear John telling him all about the transfer process, pointing to the screen to highlight his comments. John would be talking about the buildings, people and vehicles in the shot and all Ben would see was a blank screen. It was like a bitter and twisted version of Emperor's New Clothes.

He had to stop the car for a few minutes on his drive over. He'd panicked so much his shaking was threatening to crash the car. He pulled into a layby just south of Stratford, pulled out a strip of Gilly's pills; she was always taking something or other for her nerves, time to see if they worked. He popped two of the pills and swilled them down with mineral water. He had no idea what the dosage should be; he'd not checked the instructions on the box. Two should do though.

It seemed to have done the job. Twenty minutes later when he started the car engine again he felt considerably more at ease. They worked incredibly well; unless of course that was just the placebo effect. It could all be in his head. Why not? The problem itself certainly was.

~*~

John was waiting for him as he arrived and greeted him with a broad grin. 'I think you're going to like this,' he said. That line was spooky. He'd delivered it in exactly the same manner in the dream that had caused such panic in Ben. He felt a pressure building in his chest as John clicked a button on his PC causing the DVD drawer to slide open.

Ben joined him behind the counter and awaited the image to appear. After a few second he was really scared. He couldn't see anything.

John reached across and bashed the heel of his hand against the side of the PC. 'Damn piece of junk,' he said. 'Don't worry, Ben. It does this all the time. Let me pop it out and try again.' The DVD drawer slid open a second time. Ben looked at the label on the disk. Whoever John had got to do the transfer had done a great job. They'd taken a scan of the old label on the canister case and printed it onto the DVD. With that kind of attention to detail he could see why John might recommend them.

The drawer closed a second time and Ben waited once more. This time within a couple of seconds he saw Windows Media Player start on the PC and there it was. His film began playing. After just a couple of seconds John stopped it. 'The guys did a couple of versions of it to see which one you would like. This is the straight conversion. But they also did another with a typical silent movie era piano accompaniment. Would you prefer to see that one?'

Ben looked at him aghast. 'No, I don't think I would.'

John nodded. 'Good, there's still a good chunk of purist in you yet.' He winked at Ben, 'Means I might be able to sell you some more old junk. I got to make a living after all.'

He pressed play again. On the small screen the familiar scene played. Everything was as before. He could remember it all. The veil in his mind had been lifted. Ben was overjoyed. He wasn't banished.

When it ended, John popped the disk out, placed it in the DVD case and snapped the case shut. Ben's eyes were drawn to the label. They'd created a cover from superimposing the handwritten 'L'Intersezione' note, the one on the DVD itself, onto a screenshot from the film. It was a thoroughly professional looking presentation.

John slid the invoice from the company over. Ben hadn't even looked at the amount before he was handing over his credit card.

As John handed the card back and tore off the receipt he asked a further question. 'I have some other Actuality films. I found them in my store room this week. I was wondering if you might like to see them. What do you think?'

In truth, Ben didn't want them. He wasn't a convert to the genre. He was only interested in *his* film. In the week since breaking L'Intersezione he hadn't even fired up the projector, even though he owned a further six Actuality films. However,he owed this man; more than he would ever know. He nodded. John smiled and headed to the back to fetch them.

In a second he was back with twelve more films. Ben despaired. He would want to show them to him. It was a delay he didn't need. But he knew he needed this man on his side. If things went wrong again, he might need him again.

Half an hour later, he'd watched samples of four of the films and agreed to buy the lot. Another swipe of the credit card in John's machine and he waited while they were carefully packaged into their box. At least he now has something more to show Gilly if she repeats her interest in his 'latest hobby' as she put it, without having to share his prize with her. That was his alone.

Ben Williamson sat in his office staring at a computer screen full of figures. On some level of his consciousness it probably made sense but that wasn't the part of him that was functioning at this moment. He'd had the dream again last night. He'd been there.

It was better than the previous time. The rubbish, grime and damage were no more. He was rewarded with gleaming windows where the reflected sunlight threatened to prevent him seeing their contents; with smiling faces on the people occupying the streets. It was a time of joy.

But despite it being a much more agreeable experience the dream had left him exhausted. He had nearly called in sick. He could scarcely have achieved less being at home than he would today. And if he was honest, and fully aware of the facts, even Old Man Diamond would probably be happy if he didn't do anything on the Cookson accounts today, even if they had to present them for audit in four weeks. He wasn't exactly on his game. At that moment he wasn't even totally sure what that game ever was.His head was filled with the jagged lines of pain of a migraine. He couldn't think straight. The only thing his mind could focus on was the Intersection.

Last night had been a revelation. He'd been there in dreams before but not like this. Previously he'd felt he was observing as though through a haze. Last night it had been vibrant.Where everything before was muted, he saw it in vivid colours.It had shocked him.

Maybe it was because, like the film, every image he had seen of the early twentieth century was in black and white or sepia tones. So when he saw women in rich reds and blues and greens, it was magnificent.

The few men who were not working were not far behind them; although many stayed with the expected greys and dark blues, their clothes all had a wonderfully sharp style. One gentleman emerged from the subway tunnel in an immaculately tailored check suit with wide, angular lapels.And that wasn't the end of the feast his senses experienced. He could hear them. The Intersection was a real bustling, noisy place.

The first sound that had reached his dream ears was the clacking of the horses' hooves against the cobbled street. It was wonderfully rhythmic; clack, clack, clack. He closed his eyes and concentrated on its pattern. And then it was gone, hidden deep in the cacophony of sounds that was generated by the mass of traffic, both foot and vehicular; by the hawkers crying out to sell their wares; and a train passing by nearby.

And then all of a sudden he was awake. The images faded from his head quickly but the sounds lingered a while. He closed his eyes to remove the distraction of the dark shapes around his bedroom and enjoyed their sound.

One by one the noises vanished. The cars and trucks were no more. The chatter of the pedestrians faded and the cries of 'Best apples in the district' from the costermonger soon followed. Soon only the horses' hooves remained. The clack, clack, clack that had been his first auditory experience of the Intersection was the dream's final sound.It had been a wonderful experience but it had also robbed him of sleep. He'd stayed awake for the rest of the night reliving the dream in his memories.

At four thirty he'd given up on any hopes of sleep and slipped carefully out of bed. A glance backwards had told him he'd not woken Gilly. He pulled on his dressing gown and headed down to his office. He knew what he needed.By the time Gilly awoke and came down to greet him and ask about breakfast, he'd watched L'Intersezione another dozen times.

If he'd dreamed about the Intersection again that week he was unaware. Nothing woke him on any of the next four nights and no memories remained of his dreams. Much as he missed the feeling of actually being there he'd needed the recovery time. Thoroughly rested he'd even managed to catch up with the non-existence of any work on Monday and actually get ahead of his schedule. At this current rate he'd be done way before the deadline of the 28th.

He hadn't stayed away from L'Intersezione totally. He couldn't. Too many things still attracted him and puzzled him about the film. For all that it was compelling and compulsive repeat viewing, the changing nature of it troubled him. It went against everything he understood. Once something was captured on film it was trapped in time. It should be immutable. So whereas repeated watching might allow him to see details he'd overlooked before, it should not present him with a changed scene. If it was different it had to be because he'd seen it wrong the first time. But how he could he be so wrong, and so wrong multiple times.

He needed to resolve it, so he'd performed an experiment with his watching of L'Intersezione. He'd watched the DVD of the film time and time again, focussing on a single area. The new format allowed him to pause the film, and analyse the scene thoroughly. In eight viewing nothing had changed. It was the same each time. Helistened back to the recordings he'd made on his phone and compared them to the image frozen on his computer screen.

The people were as he described – a heavily moustached fat middle aged man with a slim beautiful young woman – hopefully his daughter; three children playing some kind of game with counters at the kerbside; a costermonger pushing his cart along the cobbled street. They were all as he'd remembered them; all as his descriptions had recorded them. But when it came to the buildings it was almost as though he'd seen a different scene entirely.

Except that now they were static. He'd watched the DVD transfer of L'Intersezione over and over for the past week and he could now list the stores and businesses from memory; Brennan's Butcher Shop; O'Donald's (the bar); Empire Theater (showing Burlesque).

Now that all was unchanging he'd thought again of searching for them on the internet. He should now be able to locate this Intersection. Something however had stopped him. It just hadn't felt right anymore. This place shouldn't be tied down to a street name; to a grid position or a GPS position. It was more than just a name or some numbers on a piece of paper. Knowing the facts of its geography wouldn't make this place any more real than it had been to him since the first time he'd watched the film.

The people wouldn't be any more alive. They couldn't be. It had been 106 years since the film was shot. These people's grandchildren would all be older than Ben was today. It was irrelevant. Thanks to this wonderful ten minute segment of film they would never die for Ben; they would never even age a single day. They would be there whenever he needed them. And he promised them he would visit them often.

He glanced at his watch; eleven thirty. Gilly would be back within an hour. He closed down Media Player and opened his email. He had clients to invoice.

That afternoon Ben headed into Shirley to run some errands before the shops closed. He reached the parade of shops by Solihull Road. The lights had changed to red just as he got there. Waiting gave him an opportunity to look around. If he'd made it through he would never have noticed. In the middle of all the usual suspects (fast food, charity shops, hairdressers etc.) was one shop distinctly out of place. He'd not seen it there before.

Shirley had a traditional bakery. The sign above the shop window bore the name Pullman's Bakery in old script.

It sent a chill down Ben's spine. Pullman's Bakery was a name he recognised from L'Intersezione. It was one of the shops he'd seen on the roads in his film. He stared at this one. Beyond the name they looked nothing like each other. This was a two storey building only, not the five or six that existed in the film. Shirley's version was detached; New York's connected to the buildings on either side. He was just allowing himself to be spooked.

It wasn't as though Pullman was all that uncommon a name. He'd heard it in other places after all; the train carriage; that American actor (Bill Pullman) that Gilly could never keep apart in her mind from Bill Paxton – she always thought they were the same person until he explained it to her (again). It was a coincidence but nothing more. He shouldn't read anything into it or else he'll start to turn into one of his colleagues.

Kate bought into all the conspiracy theory bullshit. If something was coincidental it meant sinister. Whenever they all went on a company night out it was an open secret that everyone tried not to sit next to Kate – especially the others who shared her office. If you were the unlucky one you would have an evening listening to her beliefs – the "*faked*" moon landings; the illuminati are running the world; pyramids are proof aliens visited the Earth millennia ago; the 9/11 towers were demolished by the US government using the terrorists as a cover. As an evening with Kate progressed the theories got more and more far fetched. But, word of advice, don't argue back; she doesn't take it well.

Ben was brought back to his present by the car horn blaring behind him. He'd not noticed the lights change. He held a hand up to apologise and moved away. He pulled off the High Street at the next exit and parked in the car park behind Aldi. All his errands were temporarily forgotten. He needed to go take a second look at Pullman's Bakery; even if only to assuage his last remaining concern. He wanted it to have no similarity to the one in L'Intersezione.

A second doubt entered his head as soon as he'd locked the car. What if the bakery wasn't there? Could he have imagined it? Could he be losing his mind? He'd thought that when he'd first noticed the changes in the film. He quickly walked back to the end of the line of shops where he'd seen the bakery, desperate to see it there and having no similarity to the Pullman's bakery in 1909 New York.

His heart was racing when he reached the shop; more from his nerves than the extra speed he'd put into his walk. He stopped in front of the window, about ten feet or so back and examined the shopfront. This Pullman's Bakery was white, brightly lit and thoroughly modern. Through the wide glass window he could straight through to the ovens behind the counter. They were continually baking in the backroom. It had nothing in common with its analogue in the film, apart from the obvious sharing of the name.

Sunday November 5th 2017, Hockley Heath, Solihull

Ben closed the file on another set of accounts. He'd decided he needed to catch up on his private work; some of the deadlines were coming due and it wouldn't be fair to risk a fine for his clients just so he could keep visiting his New York Intersection. He leant back in his chair and stretched out his shoulders.

There was one more file on his desk; Osbourne's Removals. He flicked it open. In the front sheet he saw the accounts were not due until the end of the month. He had three weeks before things became urgent. He didn't like leaving things that late normally but it could wait another day or two.

He opened up media player and started his film. The hustle and bustle of New York greeted him. The same two men walked their way down the street before heading into O'Donald's for a glass or two of the Franziskaner Beer, most likely. The advertising sign outside the bar announced it as a new German beer, never before seen in the Americas.

After about a third of the film Ben realised something wasn't quite right. It felt flat. There was not quite the same excitement as he'd had before. He was worried he might be getting bored with it. And then it came to him. There was one thing wrong.

He needed to watch the projected film not this digital facsimile. John had said something to him when he handed over the DVD copy. He mentioned some of his customers were purists; that they liked to watch these films from the original celluloid, played on the original equipment.

Ben had never thought he would be part of that category; purist. As a word he thought it synonymous with obsessive. He equated it with the people whose houses were filled with their collections to such an extent that it made it difficult to live their life amongst it all; or with those classic car drivers who dress up in period costume to drive their ancient machines.

Maybe he'd been wrong about them. Maybe there was a point to doing something right; and not just right, but totally right. He closed down Media Player, locked his computer and turned off the monitor. He needed to be in the basement watching the film on his Moviegraph.

Ben hesitated before he reached his office door. Was Gilly just beyond it in the lounge? If she was she would almost certainly ask what he was going to do. If he told her the truth she would probably want to join him. She'd enjoyed watching the other Actuality films when she'd joined him before.

He felt annoyed. He didn't ever want to share L'Intersezione with anyone else and she just wouldn't understand why this had to be his and his alone. But John had inadvertently provided him with a solution to this. He had the other box of films that he'd felt obliged to buy when he last visited John's shop. He might not have wanted them at the time but now they would serve to keep Gilly happy without him having to share his special film.

It would even heighten the anticipation. Gilly would, without any doubt, get bored after a couple of films, three at the most. Her interest in the cars and clothes of bygone times would last only a short time before the lack of any actual action lost her interest. She would head back upstairs, finding some kind of excuse so as not to make a judgment on his hobby, and he would be free to watch his film alone.

~*~

Ben had been right in every way. She'd been polishing the coffee table in the conservatory when he opened the office door. As soon as he mentioned the projector, the cleaning cloth and can of polish were discarded and the gloves tossed alongside them.

She'd watched attentively, commenting on the ladies dresses and hats as she had the first time, all through the first film. Its subject matter interested her. The camera had been set up in the lobby of a theatre and was filming people as they entered. From their thick coats and umbrellas Ben presumed it was a winter's day, and a wet one at that. The cloakroom staff members (to the left of the camera's view)were kept busy by the long queue of people depositing their outer layers before entering the theatre itself.

Ben found it almost self-referential. He'd imagined it was at venues such as this that these films would have originally been shown. He wondered whether the film makers would have had enough time during the showing of the first films of the evening to prepare this film to end the show. He had no idea what kind of process was involved between shooting and showing a film of this type? Was it like the developing of old camera film stock? He felt ashamed he hadn't spent any more time looking into the practicalities of this.

But then again, it wasn't as though he was going to go out and make his own films. These days setting up a camera to film people going out their daily business would, he imagined, result in a totally different reaction than the ones these films showed. He thought threats, both of physical violence or police involvement would happen today, especially from the parents of young children. He'd probably get branded as some kind of sick weirdo. It really was different kind of world today.

When the second film showed a football ground, Gilly
made her excuses (wanting to finish the dusting so she
could then get on with making Sunday dinner) and left.
The image large crowd gathered on a hill alongside a
football pitch. There was none of the facilities of modern
sports stadiums here.

Ben almost took the film out immediately; he had as
much of an interest in football as Gilly. But then, just as
he was reaching across to the off switch so he could stop
cranking the film, the cameraman held a board in front
of the camera. It was anything but the slick
professionalism of today's sports broadcasting. Ben
could see the hand of the cameraman in the shot.

The board announced the match being played was the
FA Cup Final of 1897.The two teams were Aston Villa
and Everton, and the match was being played at Crystal
Palace. Of course, Wembley wouldn't have existed then.
When the board was withdrawn Ben could see an image
that was mostly crowd, but with the hint of a football
pitch beyond them. It was a more a recording of the
crowd than of a football match.

Ben had never been much of a football fan but Aston
Villa had been his father's club. He didn't know the
result of this match. He knew that Aston Villa had won
the FA Cup seven times; his father used to boast
regularly about it.Ben didn't understand why. The last

time had been a decade before Ben was even born. It was hardly an indication of how good they were today.

Something happened in the film he'd not seen in an Actuality film before. Halfway through the camera moved. It was probably fairer to say the cameraman had stopped filming, moved the camera and started again. There was no neat cut. It gave the impression of it being two pieces of film joined together with no care about the join. It might be just that.

The good thing was that the new angle gave a better view of the pitch, although was still not actually targeted on the football as such. The camera had been positioned to show a wide vista across the whole ground.

Shortly after the camera angle changed a goal was scored; Ben had not the slightest idea for which team. The crowd erupted. Whichever team had scored the camera man must have been standing amongst its fans. The sound at that moment must have been incredible. Ben watched the film through to the end.

When it finished though he knew what he needed to do. He rewound the film quicker than he would normally and loaded L'Intersezione. He started winding the film and flicked on the bulb. Until the first few frames passed in front of the light Ben hadn't realised just how much he had been missing just watching the DVD transfer. This was how the film must be watched; even given the risks to the celluloid. He knew in that instance he would never watch the film on his computer again.

He scanned across the full scene. There was a life to it. It felt real. In his head he could hear the noises of the people as they went about their trades; the smells of the street filled his nostrils. The smells – that was it. He looked across to where Pullman's Bakery was – or where it had been. Where there had been baskets full of freshly baked bread for the past week, now he saw a haberdashers' shop. He looked around the rest of the screen. O'Donald's was gone too. It was still a bar but it was Dooley's Place.

Everything else that he had almost come to take for granted over the past few watchings had changed too; all except the people. They were the same people he'd seen since the very first time he'd cranked the handle on L'Intersezione. Their routines were different – you could hardly expect the woman doing her grocery run to emerge from the haberdashery carrying loaves of bread – but essentially they were all doing what they had been doing before.

His eyes landed on the theatre. The Empire Theater sign, with its surrounding lights, was no more. In its place there was the much less gaudy painted Palace Theater and Ballroom. The current attraction too had changed –

where Burlesque had been the choice for the Empire, the Palace was offering Shakespeare's Macbeth, six nights a week with a matinee on Saturdays.

Ben wasn't sure if he had expected to see the same as before. Equally he wasn't sure what he'd wanted to see. He knew though, that he wasn't freaked out by it. He wasn't even unnerved when he saw the name painted onto the glass of a door between two shops. He'd seen the door before on every viewing.

He seemed to remember it had Alexander & Sons or something like that on it before. He could listen to his recording if he needed to know – or play the DVD in his office. But all that was irrelevant. Today it said Diamond Associates. Today it shared its name with the company where he worked.

It made sense that it was there. It was his reward; his welcome back from L'Intersezione. He was accepted. Towards the end of the film a figure emerged from door. From where the camera was he had no clear view of the face of man in the trench coat and bowler hat. But he didn't need to see a face to know who it was.

As the film ended and the screen turned white, Ben was happy; happier than he'd been in days. He was back, truly back, in the world of L'Intersezione. He didn't know this would be the last time he ever watched the film.

The dream returned for Ben last night. He was among
the people of the Intersection again; where he should be.
He floated the shops, perused the items for sale inside.
He listened to the conversations between shopkeepers
and customers; to the chatter between friends passing in
the street and to the hawkers shouting out in the hope of
attracting new business.

Inside the bar he watched the men playing cards around
the tables. In back others were playing chess, dominos or
backgammon. Ben wished he could join with them. He
wanted to be the man moving his Bishop to attack his
opponent's King. He wanted to be the bridge player
winning his contract with overtricks and scoring bonus
points above the line.

A handwritten notice on a blackboard by the side of the
bar promised live music tonight. Ben wondered what
type of music it would be. It was too early for jazz, he
believed, although he knew he couldn't be sure. He
remembered the 1920s being called the Jazz Age, but
had the music existed before then? Could they have been
listening to it more than a decade earlier? And in any
case wasn't jazz a New Orleans thing? What would the
music be in a New York bar in 1909? He would have to
find out.

Outside he moved along the costermonger's barrows and carts examining the varied produce on offer. The smell of the fruit invaded his nose. It was sweeter than anything he could remember. And next was the flower stall. If anything the scents were even stronger. It was all hyper real, unlike the blandness of modern life in twenty first century Britain. For all the neon and LED brightness of Ben's world it seemed pale next to this.

When he woke from the dream he felt like a man out of place. He glanced across to the digital clock on his bedside cabinet; four thirty two. Was the dream punishing him again as it had last Monday. Was he destined for another migraine thanks to L'Intersezione?

This time though he was asleep again within a minute and when he woke with the alarm – something that never, ever happened anymore – he felt refreshed and more alive than he had in years. The normal Monday morning blues were not there. He even whistled to himself in the shower.

In the office he was cheerful; full of energy. His colleagues noticed something was different about him. He could tell from their inquisitive looks. They were all too reserved to ask. It would be different no doubt of Robyn had been at her desk when he arrived. She never had any worries about diving straight in with the difficult questions. But he'd made good time today and had beat her in.

~*~

Ben was on the top of his game. In a morning he'd brought the work on the Cookson account back on schedule; and just as well. His below par performance last week had put him considerably behind. When he had his catch up meeting with Old Man Diamond tomorrow he would be able to pull up spreadsheet after spreadsheet and report after report confirming the financial position of the firm's biggest account. Everything was going to be ready for the audit.

This would get him a bonus for sure. And he knew exactly what he needed to do with the money. He would make his first ever trip to New York. He would walk the streets and breathe in the air. He would make his pilgrimage to L'Intersezione. Even if the one in his film didn't exist – he'd come to realise that it probably never had existed outside his film – the building blocks of it were still there.

New York might have many later buildings. Much of what made up the city at the turn of the twentieth century may have been pulled down, destroyed in the name of progress; their places taken by the steel and glass skyscrapers favoured by modern thinkers and movie giant apes. But there would be a great deal of it still there. Some of the iconic buildings of today's New York must surely been there in 1909. He was fairly sure the Flat Iron Building for one predated his film, so he guessed he would find some 1909 New York still surviving.

Kate tapped on his door before opening it, 'We're popping out for lunch,' she said. 'Do you want us to get you anything?'

Ben glanced at his watch. He hadn't realised the time. Normally by this time he would be a mass of aching flesh; his shoulders would be agony; his back wound so tight from bending over his desk. Today he felt better than he had in years.

He reached into his pocket, 'That'd be fantastic,' he said in reply to Kate's question. 'Can you get me…'

He didn't finish his sentence. Kate beat him to it, 'a tuna mayonnaise baguette with salad,' she said. Ben laughed then nodded and handed over a ten pound note. He was grateful to her. He wanted to make the most of this roll he was on. He waved her goodbye and was straight back to work.

Monday November 6th 2017, Hockley Heath, Solihull

Ben suggested an early night. Gilly looked at him surprised. It was usually she that went to sleep early. She asked him if everything was okay. He made an excuse about not having slept well the night before (not true) and that he was feeling a headache starting to brew (also not true).

She looked at him; concern written all over her face. 'Just make sure you take some paracetamol and don't just sit there reading. I know what you're like. If you're tired get some sleep.'

He mock saluted as he got to his feet, 'Yes, ma'am,' he replied in a dreadful attempt at an American accent. It worked though. She laughed. It meant she wouldn't continue to try mothering him. He didn't want her to follow him.

She need not have given him the warning tonight about reading late. It may have been a habit of his to read for an hour or more after she fell asleep but tonight he was keen on being asleep and back in his dreams as soon as he was able. He was nervous when he pulled back the sheets. Would the dream allow him in tonight? He could feel his heart racing; probably not the best state to be in if you want to get to sleep.

He worried he was going to switch off the light only to lie there in the dark for the hour or so it would be before Gilly had finished watching her programmes and came to bed herself. That would make this whole effort kind of pointless. He needed to think calming thoughts. Does counting sheep work? He tried to picture cute fluffy lambs jumping over a small fence – the archetypal image for this kind of thing; the kind you see in all the kid's cartoons.

He couldn't do it. The kind of pastoral scene it required just wouldn't form in his head. It didn't surprise him; he was a city boy after all. Hockley Heath was as rural as he'd ever lived and it was semi-rural at best. There might be a farm at the end of the road where they'd bought the house, but it was hidden from view on all sides by the other houses.

The only image that would form in his head was of a certain New York street scene; the one he was desperate to return to. It was ironic that his greatest desire was keeping him from his greatest desire; ironic and somewhat typical of his warped mind. He could be the King of Contrary.

In the distance he heard a voice; followed quickly by a second. He thought it must be on the television programme Gilly was still watching. He couldn't make them out but to hear them at all meant she had the volume turned all the way up; not typical for her.

The voices just wouldn't quit. Whatever it was they sounded angry. The voices were bellowing. Ben rolled over and buried his left ear in the pillow. He hoped with only his poorer hearing ear exposed he might be able to ignore all the shouting and try to empty his mind so he could fall asleep. It didn't work. If anything the voices were getting louder.

He could almost make out words now. It wasn't argument as he'd original thought although the voices were trying to drown each other out. These were market traders calling out their prices – 'pound of fresh bacon, only twelve cents', the first voice cried. 'Chuck Steak, eight cents a pound.' A second voice offered a dozen eggs for fifteen cents.

These were the calls of the costermongers in his film. He heard them before in his dreams. He must have fallen asleep. So why couldn't he see anything? Everywhere around him was still dark. Where was the light? Where were the colours? He moved his arm. He was still in bed. He could feel the soft mattress beneath him. What was happening?

He reached out to the switch on the lamp on his bedside cabinet. His hand automatically pulled at the cord hanging down from the light shade. It puzzled him. His bedside light didn't have a pull cord. It had a switch on the central stem just below the bulb itself.

It wasn't the only thing that was different. The whole room was. The hideous wallpaper Gilly had insisted on was no more. The walls were bare, with only a coat of fading white paint covering the plaster. This wasn't his and Gilly's bedroom. He was in a hotel room in New York City, 1909. He was dreaming.

~*~

This dream was different to the ones he'd had before. He'd always been a phantom until now. He'd floated among the people but never been one of them. At this second he knew exactly who he was in this world; the world of L'Intersezione. He was still himself but he was different somehow.

For one thing he was now a resident. This room was his room. The few items he could see in it, other than the furniture, were his possessions. He lived in a lodging hotel. It was May 1909. His name was still Ben Williamson but he was not the same Ben Williamson he'd been when he fell asleep. His life here had much in common – he was still an accountant, he still worked for Diamond Associates – but it was all different.

A whole slew of new memories flowed into his mind; the memories of this world's Ben Williamson. 1909 Ben was a widower. His wife, also called Gilly, had died in childbirth, attempting to give birth to their first child. It reminded him of the complications his own wife had had. They were the reason their daughter had remained an only child.

1909 Ben's stillborn child had been a girl like his precious Naomi. He watched the memory of him holding his wife as the life leaked out of her. She'd died knowing she failed to deliver their beautiful girl into the world. It was heartbreaking.

He'd struggled on for months, trying, but ultimately failing, to recover his life. Less than a year after this Gilly's death, his double had found his way to the bottom of a bottle. He repeated it every night, only finding escape in oblivion. He lost his job. The house he and Gilly had set up together was taken from him and he found himself sleeping in the Tompkins Square Park.

Ben pulled himself out of the memories a moment. He drew a mental barrier around his mind to stop them. They were threatening to overwhelm him. He had tears running down his cheeks from reliving his analogue's life. The emotions tied into the memories were almost too strong to bear. He couldn't stop himself looking further though. Ben Williamson of 1909 New York was pulling his life together.

He allowed the memories in again. He saw a kindly old man holding a bowl of hot soup towards him. It was a cold day. 1909 Ben was shivering. The man took his coat from around his own shoulders and wrapped him in it. He sat next to 1909 Ben on the park bench and talked.

Ben felt ashamed at his expectation of a Christian bible bashing session. He thought that the man would use the soup and warm clothing as an excuse to attempt a conversion. He didn't. Mostly he just encouraged 1909 Ben to reconnect. The man didn't pry into the reasons he was here. He just wanted to help a fellow human being. Because of that one contact, that one Good Samaritan, the Ben Williamson of 1909 was able to pull himself back from the edge of destruction.

From this vantage point Ben knew his analogue had much distance to go to be fully back to normal; if that even would be possible for him. But at this second he knew the man whose body he seemed to be inhabiting was at some sort of peace. The hollowness was still there. That he knew would never leave this Ben Williamson. But he had a chance to make something of the rest of his life.

Saturday November 11th 2017, Birmingham

Ben stepped out of the train at Moor Street Station. He was in the Birmingham's city centre with Gilly. She wanted to make a start on their Christmas shopping before it got too crowded and had insisted that Ben accompany her. She announced it as soon as he had woken up; ambushed him with it before his mind had fully gotten into the day.

He'd lain in bed listening to her showering in the en suite, trying to come up with a reason why he couldn't. Nothing that she would buy into came to him. He would have claimed an appointment with one of his private clients but she'd pre-empted that. She'd told him before dropping this on him that she'd chosen today after checking the diary in his office. She knew as well as he did that if he had had an appointment he would have written it down. He was methodical like that – and old school. If he'd embraced modern technology more than he had, she'd not have been able to check. She would never have sneaked onto his office computer to check Outlook.

Gilly headed straight for New Street and Corporation Street. She'd leave the Bull Ring Centre until last, preferring to visit the shops in the older part of town before heading to the gleaming glass and steel shopping centre. Ben hoped she might find what she wanted without having to go inside the bright modern monstrosity. At least out here he could look up, above the gaudy shop fronts at the older architecture. Many of the buildings here were Victorian. Take away the neon and modern fashions from the shops and little would have changed in a century. He found the age of it oddly reassuring.

Out of the corner of his eye he saw a young boy, maybe ten years old. He looked oddly out of place. He was dressed wrong. Any ten year old today wouldn't be seen dead dressed this this. In place of the expected tee shirt, or football shirt with whoever plays centre forward for whatever team (probably Manchester United), was a woollen suit jacket. Nor was there any sign of trainers. He wore tough looking shoes; the kind Ben wouldn't be surprised to find had hobnailed soles.

The boy was holding a bundle of broadsheet newspapers and was calling out 'Tribune! Latest edition'. Ben recognised the name of the newspaper. He knew where he'd heard that before. He looked closer. It wasn't like the papers of today. There were no pictures. The whole of the front page was text. It was as much out of its time as the boy was.

He looked wider around him. The boy wasn't the only one. Here and there were others; women in flowing ankle length dresses wearing bonnets; men in three piece suits with bowler hats. And no one seemed to give them a second look as they passed through the crowd. No one other than Ben could see them.

One man walked past him, going down Corporation Street as he and Gilly we were walking up it. He doffed his hat as they passed and greeted Ben warmly. Ben returned his greeting.

Gilly stopped. 'Who were you talking to?' she asked. She turned around to look behind them. She wouldn't see him though. That pleasure was only Ben's.

'Just a colleague from work,' he said. 'I don't think you've ever met him.'

'Oh,' Gilly said. He thought for a moment she was going to ask further questions. For once though, she decided not to pry. She returned to wittering on about the day out she and her sister Ali had enjoyed yesterday. It wasn't as though she hadn't told him all this last night over dinner.

Gilly talked too much. He'd often wondered why she did. The only logical reason he'd ever been able to come up with was being afraid of the silence. If no one spoke for more than a few seconds she felt uneasy. He had no such problems. He enjoyed his own company. It was possibly one of the reasons he took on so many private clients. To Gilly he would always say it was so she didn't have to risk her health and return to work; or so they could keep Naomi in the private school. But in truth it was to have alone time; time she didn't try to fill with the inconsequential drivel that always, always, always seemed to pour forth out of her mouth.

~*~

Gilly headed into a clothes shop. Ben couldn't think of anyone she might be thinking of buying a present for from this shop. It wasn't a puzzle worth spending time thinking about. She wasn't on Christmas shopping mode really. That was much more of an excuse to come out today. This was because she wanted to buy herself things – or rather, because she wanted him to buy her things. She wasn't exactly subtle.

Ben obediently sat down on one of the chairs the store thoughtfully left out for the poor husbands and boyfriends that have to endure these experiences. He relaxed; happy to be, mostly, out of her earshot. Periodically she would appear round the end of the narrow walk space between the racks of clothes, brandishing a dress, or a skirt, or a blouse for him to comment on. Every time he tried to come up with a new non-committal phrase. It was important to not sound too in favour or against any item.

In the gaps between these mini relationship tests, Ben's attention was held by the haberdashery counter on the opposite side of the main aisle. Like the boy and the others on the street earlier, this scene was also out of its time. The assistants, all male and all dressed in trousers, shirts and waistcoats, were a blur of activity. They were giving a level of service to their customers you just don't see today. It was a world that just didn't exist anymore.

Ben regretted the time of his birth. For all the advances of modern life – including the medical treatments that could have prevented his analogue's wife from dying in childbirth – there was much to be said for life in earlier days. It was probably why he'd felt happy watching L'Intersezione and why he enjoyed his dream visits to that world as much as he did.

Everything today was fake. Everything then was real. It was as simple as that. Advances then were in the form of giant works of engineering, not digital non-corporeal things like iPhone apps. Music was people playing instruments live not downloads. People spoke in coffee shops; they didn't sit around a table texting. For all the suffering Ben Williamson of 1909 New York had gone through Ben found himself envious of him.

Gilly re-appeared with an armful of clothes. 'I'm just going to try these on,' she said. 'Are you okay there?' Ben nodded. It was an annoying question. Why wouldn't he be okay? He was a grown man, for fuck's sake. He wasn't going to cry if he couldn't see her like some spoilt snotty-nosed little shit kid.

Ben left her to it. He stood and wandered over to the Haberdashery counter that existed in another time. He crossed the barrier between 2017 Birmingham and 1909 New York. He was oddly disappointed as he made the transition. He expected to feel something but there was nothing. He glanced back behind him. 2017 was still there. He'd stepped across not knowing if he would be able to return; not knowing and not caring.

The staff behind the counter greeted him by name, 'Good morning, Mr. Williamson. It's good to see you again.' There was that service thing again. He returned their hello and exchanged a moment or two of small talk. It was a pleasant distraction from his Gilly shopping endurance test.

The head of the section made excuses and moved across to serve another customer. Ben recognised her from the film. He tipped his hat in acknowledgement of her arrival. She returned it with a nod.

His hat? He was wearing a hat. He looked down at himself. He was no longer dressed in the jeans and rugby shirt he'd left the house in this morning. He was wearing a woollen suit of an average quality. His analogue was in the process of dragging himself up but hadn't made the journey fully. The quality of cloth, or lack thereof, reflected that.

Ben's eyes wandered across to the next section of the department store. He hadn't been able to see this from his 2017 vantage point. Alongside the haberdashery was a drapery section. He walked across to check out the various fabrics available. He brushed his hands across some of the higher quality suit fabrics. It would be much better if he, or rather the Ben Williamson of 1909, wore a suit made of this fabric. Dressed properly he would probably be given control of some of that Diamond Associates better clients. He knew 1909 Ben's boss considered him capable of doing the work.

Ben greeted the assistant behind the counter and enquired about the cost of buying enough of the fabric to have a suit made. The assistant was only too eager to work out the details for him. He wrote down the figures on a piece of paper. Ben thanked him, shook the man's hand and deposited the paper in his suit pocket. He hoped his analogue would take the hint and upgrade his suit.

Just as his business there was concluded, the manager of the haberdashery section tapped him on the shoulder. 'Mr. Williamson,' he said, 'I believe your wife is looking for you.' The man pointed back through the window into 2017. He was right. Ben had seen that confused look in Gilly's face often enough.

He thanked them both and stepped back across the junction between the two times. As he went to catch up with Gilly an odd though went through his head. He was a time traveller now.

Sunday 19th November 2017, Hockley Heath, Solihull

Ben had found a neat little trick to take advantage of his double life and all thanks to that new suit. His double must have ordered it the second he returned to 2017 last Saturday. All Ben knew was that the next time he stepped across one of the bleed points – his name for the places where the two realities collided – 1909's Ben Williamson was dressed in a far better suit and his boss was calling him into his office.

When he heard the news of his analogue's promotion, Ben felt guilty he had been in his body to hear and not the man who had earned it. He hoped that the other Ben Williamson would forgive him. Old Man Diamond of 1909 was highly pleased with Ben's work and the progress he'd made recovering his life that he wanted to trust him with a bigger client and give him a pay rise, one that should see him out of the lodging hotel and into an apartment of his own again.

But it was when Ben heard which client the boss was giving him (other him) that the idea started to come together. Mr. Diamond wanted 1909 Ben to handle the Cookson account. He gave 1909 Ben the same speech Ben had heard in 2017 when his Old Man Diamond had handed the account over; word for word.

He'd thanked his other self's boss and assured him he wouldn't regret his decision – adding he would never let the firm down for good measure. And then he'd headed off to his office. The files for the Cookson account were delivered to him less than half an hour later. Ben was shocked at how much space they took up. Done the old school way the files filled six boxes.

Ben knew exactly what to look for. He retrieved the most recent box and skimmed through the paper files within for just the right one. And there it was. He pulled it out of the box and spread its contents across his computer-less desk. He was right. These were exactly the same accounts he'd been working on in 2017. He worked on them as diligently as he was able, keeping his mental fingers crossed that his hunch would be right. It was.

The next morning when he'd opened his computer files he found that all the additional work he'd done in his dream was replicated on his computer. He had no idea how that was possible or indeed why he thought it might be the case but it was exactly what he needed. He could explore his parallel life without risking the Cookson accounts being late in 2017 – or for that in 1909.

Ben scoured the classified ads in the newspaper looking for an apartment in 1909. There were quite a number available within his price range but only one that was an option for him. Only one of the buildings was in one of the buildings around the Intersection. It was fate; meant for him. A few months ago he would never have believed anything was down to fate – it was all just coincidence. But then, a few months ago he wouldn't have believed in time travel or parallel lives either.

And surprisingly there was a telephone number listed for enquiries. That must have been almost unheard of in 1909.He asked Mr. Diamond for permission to use the company telephone to make the call. The old man was only too happy to allow him to do so, on the condition that he work out the cost of the call and reimburse the company – he was an accountant after all.

Ben made the appointment for his analogue. With any luck by the next time he visits this world he would be waking up in his own apartment. He would have his own bathroom and not have to queue for his turn with the shared facilities of the lodging hotel.

Ben Williamson was living the perfect life. He had the perfect balance. He lived his days in 2017, with occasional trips through a bleed point, then, when he went to sleep would wake up instantly in his double's body in 1909 New York.

He was surprised he wasn't tired. He hadn't actually slept in weeks. He wasn't though; he felt more alive than he could remember ever feeling. Maybe it was something to do with *it*, the mechanism or magic that made all this possible. Whatever it was he wasn't going to complain.

Gilly had started to notice he was sleeping more. She was nagging him to go see a doctor and just wouldn't quit. It was bugging him more and more. He'd started staying out after work; one of the bars in town bled into Dooley's Place; and Dooley's Place seemed to always be open. He'd never crossed over to find it closed.

When he thought about it he'd never been in New York 1909 when anything was closed. Time there and here didn't quite seem to marry up. The days seemed to pass at the same rate; every time a day passed in 2017, one did in the past. But it wasn't quite a linear thing. They just didn't do it at the same rate. Again it was something he wasn't going to question as long as it did it in a way that suited him.

More and more he'd found the people he knew in 2017 had doubles back then. He supposed what he did could be done by any of them. Well maybe except Gilly; her analogue was still dead. That transfer was one he wasn't sure you could survive. And if you could what kind of experience would it be, trapped in a coffin in a decaying corpse. But her aside it seemed others could experience what he did.

He'd tried questioning some of them; wanting to know if he was alone in living both sides or not. No one though had responded as he would have expected if they were a time travel like him. Robyn on reception at Diamond Associates had thought he was losing it when he tried. She'd replied in her overly loud thick Brooklyn accent that maybe he should ease down a little – maybe get some rest. He'd given up trying after that. He didn't want to ruin this by being labelled a kook (Robyn's word).

In any case he wasn't sure it mattered. All that did was that what he had was real and it didn't go away. It was why he'd stayed diligent to his work. He wasn't allowing the many temptations to spoil it. Solihull was awash with bleed points. There was even one in the office; in the main conference room. It led through to the store room behind his office in 1909.

He'd used it once or twice, usually from 1909 when access to a computer would speed up the work he was doing back then. But other than that he was sparing. He didn't want to do anything that could risk upsetting this balance. Gilly though was about to change everything.

~*~

It was just four short words; 'I want a divorce'. He hadn't been expecting that. He'd asked her why; repeatedly. He'd had to; she wouldn't answer him at first. Then she'd said it. She *knew* he was having an affair. He'd laughed when she said it. That hadn't helped matters any. She went nuts.

He'd spent the next half an hour trying to calm her down. He asked her why she thought this. 'It's all the long hours,' she'd said, 'I know you're not working, so what else can it be?' She was referring to the times he spent in the other time before coming home. And if she knew he wasn't working she must be checking up on him. 'And when you do come home you're straight to bed. There has to be a reason you're always so tired.'

That was a problem; he really didn't have an excuse that would be even remotely believable. He could hardly say he was living a second life in New York City a hundred years ago. She'd might give up on the divorce and just seek to have him committed.

He tried to reason with her. He denied the affair of course; easy to do as there wasn't one to complicate matters. She wanted to know what he was doing with those times after work before he came home. And she wasn't going to take no for an answer. Then a way out of it came to him.

'I've got a hobby,' he said.

'A hobby?' She didn't sound convinced. 'But if that's all it is, why didn't you tell me?'

'It's a little embarrassing.' He tried to sound a little sheepish. If what he was about to *admit* was true, he knew he would be sheepish about it. 'I've taken up salsa dancing. There's a class for beginners in town. I go there after work.'

'You what?'Her voice showed he complete shock.

'One of the ladies at work, Candy, goes,' (true). 'She says it's a great way to keep the pounds off without having to go jogging or hit the gym. And I am getting a bit older.'

'But Salsa Dancing? It just doesn't sound like you.' She still looked a little dubious. 'Why should I believe you? This sounds all too far fetched.'

'I can show you.'

'Just having the costume in a bag in the boot of your car won't convince me. You could have been planning this excuse for weeks for all I know.'

'But if you saw me doing Salsa Dancing, would that do it?'

Gilly hesitated a second. 'It might. But you can't surely be going every night? You're late home pretty much all the time recently.'

'It isn't, you're right. I've been using a laundrette to wash my dance clothes. I didn't want to risk my secret getting out.'

She looked at him but didn't reply. She wasn't buying it. There was doubt all over her face. But equally she wasn't dismissing his story out of hand. It probably helped that one of the women at work did go Salsa Dancing.

'Look,' he said, taking her hands in his. 'Before we let this misunderstanding get out of hand and wreck everything, let's meet up in town one night after I leave work…tomorrow, and you can come along and see.'

'I don't know.'

'Just give me a chance to prove my innocence. After all these years surely I deserve that.' He said. When she said nothing he added, 'I'll take you out for a meal afterwards. I'll book a table at that restaurant you like.'

She nodded her agreement. 'Okay, I'll give you a chance. But tonight you sleep in the guest room. I'm not sure I trust you anymore.'

'If that's what you want, Gilly,' he said.

Ben was glad his double life had given him the time to get ahead of the work on the Cookson account. It gave him all the time he needed for his preparations. He took care of the basics in the morning. He booked the table at the restaurant. Gilly was predicable enough to check. He researched enough about Salsa Dancing to answer any questions she might come up with; he was just glad she hadn't thought to do that last night. He would have been stumped by even the easiest of question.

At lunch he headed out of the office to buy the kind of outfit he might be expected to wear Salsa Dancing; and then spent an hour back in his office trying to make it look used.

He placed most of his new possessions into his holdall. He could pull it out later to show her, backing up his story. Then he would drop his bombshell on her.

He would play the martyr, the injured party card as hard as he could. He'd claim to be upset at her lack of trust in him. And then *demand* that she join him in the class. Gilly hated being put on the spot like that. She had no backbone. She would try to protest, to refuse the *offer*, but she would give in easily. And that's when he would play his trump card. He just hoped he was right about it all. He couldn't see why it wouldn't work.

Ben glanced at his watch; three pm. It was two hours until he could legitimately leave the office. He just wanted this to be over and done with. He hated waiting around; he certainly wasn't in the mood to do any work. But he couldn't just leave. It would be jus this luck if Gilly rang to check if he was there and not with this imaginary mistress she'd created.

He actually regretted not having one. It would have made all this stress just a little easier to deal with. And it wasn't as though he hadn't had the chance. Back in 1909 there was this woman who had a definite interest in him. She wasn't even subtle about it. He'd held back because he didn't know what effect that would have on his double's life.

It wouldn't be fair to saddle him with a jealous husband out for his blood; especially as if the guy turned out to be the violent type, well…you just didn't know what might happen. A moment's fun on his part might result in the death of his double; and that would end his 1909 life.

It was why he'd steered clear of the bars around the Intersection even though he would love to taste the beers of old New York. Leaving the taste of it on his double's tongue, and the buzz in his head, might return him to his bad old habits. He didn't fancy living the life of a down and out.

~*~

Finally the clock ticked over to five pm. Ben waited a few more minutes until he heard the exiting of his colleagues. Today was not a day for anything appearing out of the ordinary and his leaving exactly on the dot of five was something people would notice.

Ten minutes was as much as he could stand to delay things. He grabbed his coat and briefcase and headed for the carpark. He said quick hellos the few staff remaining in the building. Fortunately none of the company gossips were still around. He managed to get out within a couple of minutes.

Autumn was definitely in full swing now. The relatively warm weather earlier in the month had gone. The wind was blowing strongly. It wafted the bottom of his coat upwards. As he reached his car, it was starting to rain; not a problem. He stowed his briefcase in the back of the car, pulled his coat lapels up around his neck and headed to the pub where he'd asked Gilly to meet him. He'd be in the dry in no more than a minute.

Gilly though might get a little wet as she made her way across from the main shopper' car park at Touchwood. The thought of it brightened his spirits a touch; it served her right for the grief she'd caused him last night.He bought two drinks at the bar and settled down at a table that gave him a great view of the bar and waited.

Ten minutes later and Gilly walked in. He waved her across and pushed the gin and tonic to her side of the table. He was going to do his best to make this feel as amicable as it could after her drama queen moment last night. He didn't want her to suspect a thing. He was going to be the perfect husband right this second.

She thanked him for the drink and sat down opposite. It looked like she was wary of him. Normally she would have pulled a chair around to next to him. She liked physical contact. Tonight though she was making the table into a barrier; or maybe he was reading too much into it. Whatever, it didn't really matter all that much.

He allowed her a couple of swallows from her drink and a minute or two of awkward small talk before playing his card. 'Gilly, I want you to know that you're not trusting me was upsetting.' – A lie.

'You didn't give me much reason to trust you,' she replied. Good, she's defensive, he thought.

'But did I give you any reason to actively distrust me? And did you give me a chance to say anything before jumping straight to asking for a divorce.'

'But…' he didn't allow her to answer. This wasn't her time.

'Let me finish first,' he interrupted. 'I have put up with being the sole earner in the family now for more than a decade so you could not have to work after what happened.'

'I know and…' He held a hand up to stop her again.

'And haven't I sacrificed my Sundays for the past five years so we could afford to send Naomi to that private boarding school you wanted her to go to?'

'I guess so, yes,' she admitted.

'Guess? There's no guess in this. The answer you are looking for is "Yes"; pure and simple.' He raised his voice a little with this last sentence. One or two heads in the pub turned towards them. That would help. She hated being the centre of attention.

'Gilly, I have put everything into this marriage; everything. If I was willing to put in that much effort, wouldn't you have thought it was because I wanted it to succeed? Why would I do all that only to cheat on you?'

Gilly looked flustered; good. 'I don't know,' she admitted.

'So now do you understand why I'm upset at you?' He asked. Gilly nodded. He could see a tear forming in the corner of her eye, right, now to reel it back in a little. He needed her to feel he was on her side.

'Gilly, I want you to know that you are the only woman I have ever loved, and the only woman I have slept with since we met. That hasn't changed any and I don't want it to change for as long as we both live.' That got the tears flowing, although it also brought a smile to her face.

'I am willing to accept some of the blame here,' he continued. 'I shouldn't have been so hesitant to tell you about the class. I just didn't want anyone to know. It seemed a little wrong. But I should have known I could tell you anything. Will you forgive me for that?'

Gilly nodded. She croaked out a 'yes'.

'Well, tonight I am going only to prove my words to you but I want to share my hobby with you.'

'You want to what?' she exclaimed.

'I want you to come along with me.'

'But I don't know anything about Salsa Dancing,' she protested.

'That's not a problem. Do you really think I do after four weeks? It's only a beginners' class.'

'I can't do it in these,' she said, pointing down to the clothes she was wearing.

'I know,' he smiled, trying to reassure her. 'But we can take care of that. I took a walk out at lunchtime. The department store by the office sells everything you might need.' He finished his drink. 'Come on, let's go shopping.'

~*~

Ben had expected to feel remorse as the moment of his plan approached. He'd gone over and over how to do this in his mind since Gilly had asked for the divorce yesterday, and for all that it made sense he wasn't sure he would be able to go through with it.

But as they were standing on the escalator as it took them upwards towards the department he needed, Gilly was obligingly reinforcing his decision. She was whittling.

'What if I'm no good at it?' – It doesn't matter.

'They probably won't have anything to fit me?' – They will.

'What if someone sees me?' – So what.

He walked her towards the ladies clothing section. So far so good. Just as they passed the first of the rails of clothes (nothing suitable for Salsa Dancing on this rack), he took hold of her hand and turned them right between the racks. She was surprised at the contact, but didn't pull away. That was good. If she had withdrawn her hand he would have had to manhandle her. He would have if necessary but this was easier. Holding her hand and walking, like any normal married couple, was much better.

He smiled and laughed as they approached the bleed point. She was halfway through asking what was so funny when they crossed into 1909. The question was never finished. Ben now stood alone; his hand was empty.

He turned around to look back into 2017 to see if she'd remained there. There was no one behind him. He crossed back and looked all around. Gilly was nowhere to be seen. It had worked.

Ben was laughing as he put the remainder of his plan into operation.

As Ben walked into the office, Robyn accosted him. She was desperate to know if there was any news about Gilly; they all were. He apologised to her for having none. He even managed to keep his face downbeat. It was a struggle as all he wanted to do was celebrate every moment of freedom.

Robyn was quickly joined by Kate and the others. They had been doing this every morning since the news of Gilly's disappearance had reached them. They all thought he was coping so well. He wished they would just leave him alone. Robyn was like an overbearing mother hen at the best of times; give her an actual crisis, even if it was one he didn't trouble over, and she was unbearable. He made an excuse of wanting to be left alone to get on with it; saying he needed normality at the moment to take his mind off things.

Robyn took this as truthful. He'd expected nothing less. She was so gullible; Kate too. Kate even backed him when he mentioned the police had interviewed him as a potential suspect. Routine, he told her he thought it was; typical of the system's incompetence, her view.

She was as wrong about that as she was about everything. From his perspective the police were being extremely professional and extremely considerate. It was true that they'd questioned him about his part in her disappearance but they'd explained it was just a formality. They had to get his side to see if it tied into the evidence they had.

It had. He'd made sure of it. He'd crossed over with Gilly in one of the places where the shop's security cameras wouldn't get a clear shot; the reason he'd chosen the old department store and not the newer shops in the Touchwood Centre was its poorer coverage. Once she was gone he'd then made sure his face was seen clearly on several of the cameras.

He'd taken the expected husband position, seated near the racks of skirts, not far from the changing rooms; exactly what would be expected of a man accompanying his wife on a clothes buying trip. He'd taken out his Evening Mail and started reading through the headlines.

After twenty minutes he'd glanced at his watch then stood and scanned the aisles. Just in case the cameras were sensitive to see faces clearly he'd put on a puzzled expression. He was acting his heart out. A further fifteen minutes of alternating between his paper and looking around and he'd put the final part into operation. He'd gone to search for an assistant.

The young woman he'd found had been incredibly helpful. She checked in all the changing rooms while he waited outside; then did the same for the ladies toilets on the floor. For good measure she even checked all the toilets on every floor. By the end of her search she was almost as distraught at not finding her as he was pretending to be.

She hung around while he called the police on his mobile. The man who answered listened to him patiently as he read through his script, before giving Ben the response he expected, 'Could she have just done a runner, Sir?' he'd asked. 'Maybe she just left.'

He suggested he go home (she might be there) and call her friends and family. 'One of them will probably know where she is,' he'd added. They wouldn't. No one would again. He ended the call with an instruction to call them again tomorrow if she hadn't returned.

They all took this as him being the poor abandoned husband. All except Gilly's sister, Ali, that is. She all but accused him of her murder the last time they met. They'd never been on the best of terms. He'd never been totally sure why and didn't care any longer. He wouldn't have to see her any more.

Naomi had been the one tricky part of it all. He'd not really thought what it might do to her when he "*disappeared*" her mother. He'd driven up to her boarding school as soon as he'd finished with the police.

He didn't want her to find out over the telephone. That would have been callous.

He'd told her in the headmistress's office. She'd half collapsed to the floor when he told her. She shared too much of her mother's frailties for his liking. He'd brought her back home straight after that. She'd wanted to be there when her mother called. She'd waited forlornly every day. That almost broke Ben.

Ben Williamson wasn't looking forward to his first Christmas without Gilly.It wasn't that he was all of sudden missing his wife. He didn't think that would ever happen. His problem was his daughter. She'd been home since her mother disappeared, the school granting her compassionate leave or some crap like that, and it was becoming tiresome. With her around it was trickier to get to his bleed points and get his quick fix of 1909 during the day.

He'd still have the nights; he knew that. But he liked the extra time he sneaked in during the day. With Naomi close and hand and worse, all the places where he'd discovered the places where he could cross between worlds, the shops and pubs, as well as his office, would be closed. Even when they reopened he would be obliged to spend time with his daughter; she was grieving after all. For the best part of a week he would be denied them.

So he'd decided he needed to make the most of the chances he would have before he shutdown began. And today was the first of them. He'd booked the day off work – telling Diamond he wanted to start getting the house ready for Naomi; try to make it as much of a Christmas for her as was possible in the circumstances.

132

It sounded good and the old man had bought every word. He probably hadn't needed to lay it on quite so thick. After the audit of the Cookson account had gone so well, Diamond would have allowed him the time off even without such a good sounding reason. He was deeply in Ben's debt he'd said. The firm owed a lot to him.

Obviously not enough to hand out a big bonus for all his good work though. Ben guessed you don't get to own a villa in the South of France where you spend every weekend if you hand out money to people when they do their jobs. At least Diamond's analogue in 1909 had done the decent thing. His work in both the times had earned his double a healthy bonus; enough to fully furnish his apartment – as long as he stuck to the thrift stores, that is.

Ben headed for his favourite pub. He was becoming something of a regular; enough for the bar maid to greet him as he walked in. The pub had a good reputation for keeping beer well, but Ben had not tested it. Since starting to share his analogue's life Ben had abstained from alcohol. He didn't know whether tasting it here would filter across the worlds but it wasn't a chance he was willing to take. Why risk upsetting the applecart?

The thing that kept Ben coming back time and time again was the bleed point. The corridor that led to the pub's back door – the one leading to the car park – was his passage through to 1909. It was ideal. He could pop in, have a (soft) drink or two, make conversation then head home. It was perfect; far less suspicious than using the one he knew existed in the lingerie shop.

~*~

Ben Williamson stepped into the yard behind Dooley's. He greeted the men unloading the barrels of beer from the cart. They tipped their hats back at him. He pulled his coat up tighter around him. It was a bitterly cold day in New York; certainly not one he'd like to be working outside in like these guys.

He stubbed out his cigarette and thought about heading into the bar. Given 1909 Ben's alcoholism that would not be good; even if he could guide him straight to the exit. It might linger in his subconscious; make him think he had control over it and that he was safe to give it a try. That was one slippery slope not to risk. His double even being here, outside the bar, was dangerous.

He wondered how the continuity worked. Each of the bleed points in 2017 led to a specific place in 1909. The Ben of this time was always in the right place every time he came across; no matter whether it made sense for him to be there. If it looked odd to anyone no one mentioned it. Ben chalked it up as another of those things it was best for him not to ask about. Be glad that it worked and don't sweat it. He stepped around the front of the cart, patting the horse on the neck as he did so.

He knew just where he needed to be; the coffee house. He wasn't sure whether it was a lingering puritanism that kept this place going or just that coffee was still enough of an exotic luxury that drew people here, but he was glad they came. It was the interaction with people that Ben enjoyed most about being in this New York; even if was just listening in to Mrs. O'Malley's gossiping.

'You know me,' she'd say in her thick Irish accent. 'You know I'm not one for gossip.' Not one, he thought, more like Number One. Then she'd start. She seemed to have something to say about every family on the block.

Today though, his interactions didn't have to be passive. Old Tom was in. Tom was a fanatical chess player. Ben had probably played thirty games with him since he started coming here; and old Tom had won every one. Ben didn't care. He wasn't here to start a career as a chess grandmaster.

It was through Old Tom that Ben learned most of the truly useful information he had about 1909 in New York. He didn't have the background knowledge that a lifetime living in this city would have given him. So Old Tom was his information trove. If the old guy thought it funny that Ben kept asking all these questions he didn't say anything. Maybe he just liked the fact he had someone to play (and beat) at chess. It also helped that Ben covered his drinks and food bill on each of these encounters.

Ben pushed a pawn out two spaces to start the game. Old Tom quickly responded in similar fashion. And just like that they were off. This was going to be a good afternoon.

~*~

After three quick defeats to Old Tom, Ben had thrown in the towel. He could have played another – his victorious opponent would have no doubt been happy to play him again – but Ben wanted to walk amongst the people on the streets. He had made a number of friends amongst the market traders, especially a recent immigrant from Naples called Giuseppe – or Pep. It probably helped that Ben knew a reasonable amount of Italian. Pep liked having the chance to use his native language.

As soon as he rounded the corner, heading back to the market stalls Ben noticed that something was oddly different. It suddenly occurred to him that since he'd found out how to cross over and visit the Intersection in person it had become static. After all those viewings of the film, with the every changing businesses and shops, he was amazed it hadn't occurred to him before. He realised he'd not watched the film once since he learned how to cross over. Maybe that's why Dooley's had stayed Dooley's; and Luigi's and the Palace Theater.

Now though there was something new. On the opposite side of the street was a narrow shop with all kinds of oddments arrayed outside and in its window. Above the door was a simple sign – Clyde's Curios. It was a junk shop.

Ben wanted to go check it out. Something felt odd about it though. It looked familiar. That sounded stupid. So much of this place was identical to back home, why should a junk shop spook him? After meeting more than thirty identical(-ish) copies of people from his time here, now he gets the willies. He shook his head admonishing himself and headed across the road, avoiding the chaos of the late afternoon and, maybe more importantly, the piles of horse shit littering the street.

He stopped outside Clyde's curios and examined it thoroughly. This was exactly the kind of shop he dreamed of finding back in 2105, the kind that was sadly now (then) mostly extinct. It was almost as though it was too good to be true. Now he really was scaring himself; ridiculous, it's just a shop.

He reached for the handle and headed inside. Inside it was a mass of every possible doohickey and what chamacall it you could imagine. It was like someone had taken the curiosities cabinet he kept in his home office and upscaled. He would have to be careful or he could spend his double's entire paycheck in here inside an hour.

After a few minutes of sensory overload Ben heard a noise from the back of the store. A man emerged from the back room. Ben had become so inured to the ways of the Intersection that his being a copy of John, the dealer who had sold him the Moviegraph and started this whole thing off, didn't phase him one bit.

He'd also become so blasé about it that he didn't even think of trying to see if John was a time traveller like him. So when John greeted him by name it actually made Ben jump. 'Hello Ben.' Two simple words; two simple words that freaked the living shit out of Ben.

'John?' Ben asked.

'The one and the only. Long time no see, Benny boy.' John looked rather more serious than his jocular words. 'We have got to talk, Benny.' Ben felt a chill run up and down his spine.

Ben had expected to have to put on the performance of
his life to make people think he was struggling to get
through the first Christmas without Gilly. He hadn't had
to. In fact he hadn't to act at being miserable for the past
two weeks; he was miserable. John had given him the
worst choice imaginable. And to make it worse until he
made the decision he was not allowed to travel between
times.

It seems he was wrong about one thing – there were
rules about what you could do and he'd broke one of
them. He just wished someone had told him. Ben had
listened to everything John had had to say, and then he
had lied through his teeth to him in reply.

He'd laid it on pretty thick. He wanted to share this with
his beloved Gilly. He wanted her to share the experience
with him. Imagine his anguish when she disappeared. He
didn't know what had happened. John gave him that
look; the one that said he wasn't totally convinced. At
least he wasn't dismissing Ben's story out of hand as it
deserved.

'Okay,' he said finally. 'Let's presume that I believe
you. It doesn't explain your behaviour over the time

since you *accidentally* killed your wife. You haven't exactly been a dictionary definition of grieving husband.'

'I didn't think she was dead,' he'd claimed. 'I thought she'd slipped her hand from mine just before we crossed and then simple run away.'

'Without her car?' John asked. 'You do know the police found it where she'd parked in the Touchwood car park?'

Ben claimed he wasn't exactly thinking straight. He repeated over and over he didn't know what would happen and how it had been a terrible accident. He was sorry. He wished he could go back and do it all again. This time he would do things differently, he promised. He pleaded with John to allow him to go back.

When John told him that kind of thing wasn't possible, that the two times on either end of the portal were locked together and could not be manipulated as he suggested, Ben collapsed to the ground. He even managed to get tears flowing on cue.

John hesitated, looking at him a moment or two longer, then dropped his own bombshell. 'They've decided you can't live in both times any more,' he said. Ben had no idea who this "*they*" were. They sounded important though. 'You have to choose one of the worlds and live there and only there. No more crossing.'

Ben hadn't believed what he was hearing. He'd asked John to clarify it. It was true. Ben could return to his time or stay here today. But then he would have to choose which. Then he would live permanently in 2017 Solihull or 1909 New York.

Ben had got it together long enough to ask how much time he would have. Two weeks was the reply. And that had been thirteen days ago. He had to choose between the advantages the twenty first century gave him – better medical care, advanced technology, a more comfortable life in general – or the excitement and adventure that 1909 New York would provide. He would also have to choose between a life which featured his daughter and one that didn't.

He put his accountant brain into the task; creating a pros and cons spreadsheet to help him decide. It was a close call but in truth he'd always known the way it was going to go. He'd never felt more alive or happier than when he travelled back. New York was the only option he could make.

He hugged Naomi for one last time. She was going down to Wiltshire to spend New Year's with a school friend. It was perfect timing on her part. He drove her to New

Street station, wished her as happy a New Year as she could possibly have and waved her off. Her train left the station and he drove back to Solihull to travel back for the final time.

Despite the holiday season the Stratford Road was a mass of cars, lorries and buses. He wouldn't miss this aspect of the twentieth century. There might be as much traffic as this in 1909 but the handcarts and the horse drawn wagons were quainter.

He drove back to Solihull and headed straight for his favourite pub. This was one thing he would miss about this time. If you discounted his smart phone this place might be top of his miss list. He lingered in the pub longer than he normally would. He wanted to make the most of this final opportunity to be part of this community.

But eventually he knew it was time. He said his goodbyes; repeated Happy New Years so many times he lost count and kissed most of the women (and one of the men) on the cheek. The barmaid had even swivelled her head at the last minute so that kiss fell squarely on her lips. Why couldn't she have done that before he'd made this decision? Too late now.

With one final look back he headed down the corridor and stepped into the yard behind Dooley's Place. Winter in New York was horrific. The wind was howling through the alleyway, blowing the snow horizontally. It stung as it hit his face.

He glanced at 1909 Ben's watch. It was mid-afternoon; not that you would believe it. He quickly headed around the corner and ran across to Clyde's Curios. He was surprised to see the market stall holders were out despite the season and the weather. He guessed they didn't have the option the way their counterparts in 2017 might. He waved across to Pep as he bolted for Clyde's and the warmth within. On the corner diagonally opposite he didn't notice the two men setting up a movie camera. The film had started to roll as he entered the shop.

John was waiting for him inside. 'So Benny Boy, you made your decision?'

Ben nodded. 'I have,' he said.

'So which is it to be? 2017 or 1909?'

'1909,' Ben said simply in response.

'You do surprise me,' John replied. 'I didn't think you would give up all the luxuries of modern life; or your daughter.'

'Some things are more important,' Ben replied.

'I guess so.'

'So what do we have to do now? Is there some kind of ritual you want me to undergo?'

'No, heaven forbid. Nothing so supernatural.' John held out a hand. 'All it takes it a handshake and the deal is done. You will take your double's place and live to the end of your days in 1909.'

Ben took the man's hand and that's when it all changed. In front of his eyes decay set in. Corruption infected everything.

'What the fuck?' Ben asked. 'John, what have you...?'

'Hey, don't blame me Benny Boy. You were the one looking at things through those rose coloured glasses of yours. Now you're part of this world they're being taken off.' John started to laugh and disappeared into the back room.

Ben went back out into the street. The corruption had beaten him to it. The streets looked as run down as the dream he'd had when the film had snapped. He'd thought at the time it was his subconscious punishing him for his clumsiness but it was more than that, he knew now. He'd been given a warning of the reality of this world and he'd chosen to ignore it.

He looked right and let trying to find something that would bring hope back. There was nothing. The street was pitted with holes; the few businesses that remained open were obviously on their last legs with broken windows either covered with boards or left as they were, jagged glass and all, allowing the cold winter to penetrate inside.

He pulled his coat tight around him hoping it would keep out the wind. It was more threadbare than it had been when he entered John's shop. Pulling it tight ripped it a little further, lessening its protection rather than increasing it. As he ran back across the road towards Dooley's Place a fight broke out. Ben saw a flash of steel before the knife was buried in Pep's ribs. He was dead before he hit the cobblestones. No one moved to help him. Two young boys ran off, presumably taking his friend's takings with them.

He pulled at the door of Dooley's hoping to gain entrance. It wouldn't budge. Old Tom passed by, 'I wouldn't bother with that, Mister,' he said. 'I can't see it opening any time soon after those thugs put Dooley in the hospital.'

'Why did they do that?' Ben asked.

'Guess Dooley got fed up paying the protection money,' Old Tom said. He took a swig from his bottle. 'Idiot –

it's better being a poor man than a dead man.' He wondered off.

Ben was terrified. What had he done? What fate had he brought upon himself? John had played him for a fool. He needed to escape. And he had just the way to do it. He checked his pockets. He had money. He ran to the subway entrance and quickly descended the stairs leading down. He'd expected to find a subway station. He knew they existed in 1909. Whether this one had ever been open though, it certainly wasn't now. The concourse, far from being the bright open space with gleaming tiled walls and floors, was a black hole. The stairs went nowhere.

He climbed back to street level and looked along the roads. Nothing existed beyond the extent of L'Intersezione. Diagonally across from where he stood, he finally saw the two men taking the camera down. He called across to them. In the near howling gale they didn't hear him. They headed off towards the blackness.

Ben sprinted across the street, dodging the rabid looking horses and potholes as he went, trying to catch them up. All the time he screamed out to them, but they just didn't hear him. He was less than an arm's length away when they disappeared into the blackness. He was trapped.

~*~

John shook 1909 Ben Williamson's hand. 'So do you think you're going to be alright?' he asked him. 'You are a century out of date after all.'

'I think I'll be okay,' Ben replied. He'd learned a lot in his previous visits to the twenty first century; this internet thing was a revelation. He could find out anything he might want to know in an instant. With that and the additional help John had promised him he knew he would be okay. His counterpart from this world had freed him. Ben couldn't believe anyone would give all this up, even though John had always told him it was a done deal, right from his first meeting with 2017 Ben.

'What are you going to do next?' Ben asked him.

John laughed. 'The same again I guess. Only this time I am going to go somewhere warmer. England in December is too cold for me. What about you?'

'Well, I'm looking forward to getting to know my daughter,' he replied.

Ben shook John's hand one last time and headed out of the pub into the cold December air. John sat at his table watching him go. He pulled a world map out of his pocket and took a drink as he scanned it. 'Somewhere warmer,' he muttered to himself.

John, no it was Juan now, lifted another crate of knick-knacks to the counter top. He enjoyed this part more than just about any of the rest of it. He liked the set up as much, if not more than the catch up. He was a stickler for preparation. Everything had to have its place. And the whole had to look almost organic.

This only worked if his customer believed the store had been there for longer than a few days. He didn't know why but it just seemed to be the case. He checked himself in the mirror. He'd got his look about right too. He had to match the aged look of the store after all. If anyone looked closely they would see he was not quite right. But who ever looked closely at the old guy who ran an antiques shop.

When he was nearly down to the bottom of the final crate he smiled. There it was. He lifted the dull metal canister from the crate and looked around the shop. Where was the best place for it? It had to be half hidden but easy to see. He needed the customer to see it and believe he'd discovered a long lost treasure.

His next customer would be in later. He knew who it would be already. It worked like that for him. This next guy was a lot like Ben. He was as unhappy with his lot and as likely to jump all in when offered an exciting new life. There was a type, John had come to see. You could spot them a mile off.

He wondered at times whether he should feel sorry for them, but he just didn't. Why should he? Over the years he'd been doing this nearly every single one had given in to their baser natures. Ben's killing of his wife had hardly been the first spousal murder he'd seen.

John/Juan sat down in the chair behind the counter and waited. It wouldn't be long now. Just as he'd closed his eyes, he heard the bell notifying him that the door had opened.

The End

1920 Keystone MOVIEGRAPH Hand-Crank 35mm MOVIE
PROJECTOR - Model 575

Table of Contents

www.ingramcontent.com/pod-product-compliance
Lightning Source LLC
Chambersburg PA
CBHW021059130626
46552CB00005B/2185